IF ONLY I'D KNOWN

IF ONLY I'D KNOWN

Jenny Davis

ORCHARD BOOKS

For Christine and for John

ORCHARD BOOKS
96 Leonard Street, London EC2A 4XD
Orchard Books Australia
14 Mars Road, Lane Cove, NSW 2066
Originally published in the United States in 1988
by Orchard Books
First published in Great Britain in 1989
as SEX EDUCATION
This edition published in 2000

A CIP catalogue record for this book is available
from the British Library.
1 84121 789 1
1 3 5 7 9 10 8 6 4 2
Printed in Great Britain

0

PROLOGUE

This is a story I would rather not tell. It is a stick caught in my throat, gagging me, choking its way up, and now I am stuck with it. I don't want to tell it, but Hirsch says I must and Hirsch is my doctor. He says there is healing in telling, telling even the worst. But what he doesn't understand is that I don't want to get well. So. There. Now I've said it.

My name is Olivia Sinclair. I am sixteen years old. I am writing this at my desk in my room on the ninth floor of the University Psychiatric Institute. This is where I now live. I've been here for an entire year, which is something of a record for this place. You're supposed to get well and go home or get worse and go to State. From what I hear, the state hospital is a real pit. This place is not. Actually, it's very nice. Rugs, curtains, windows.

Outside of my window is the stadium. Nine storeys up I can see over part but not all of the stadium wall. Last fall, when football season started, I heard the band practising over there. I could hear them marching up and down, playing music, and the band director stopping them, yelling at them. Then on the weekends I could hear the games and see the people. People, thousands of them, screaming. Now there is no one. It is February. That makes it a year.

I hold another record of sorts here — for being the youngest person on the floor. It's not a bad thing; the nurses and many of the other patients treat me as if I'm some kind of pet. People give me candy although I don't eat it. One woman pinches my cheek every time she sees me. I avoid her. There are younger people in the hospital but I am the youngest on the ninth floor.

I was fifteen when I came. I really don't remember it. Hirsch says I couldn't open my eyes and I couldn't talk, or at least I didn't. He isn't sure which. Mostly I slept. For seven months. And then, five months ago, I opened my eyes and looked around and saw my room here and found out where I was.

And I remembered. I remembered all of it and wished then that my eyes were still shut and that I could be senseless once again. It hurt. It hurt to remember, to know. It still does.

At first, after I opened my eyes and tried to speak, the words came out all slurred and jumbled — glumph ab ooj eenka. Nothing made sense. I could understand what people were saying to me but I couldn't say anything back that was recognisable. Hirsh put me on drugs then, three tranquilisers a day and a sleeping pill at night. They make my tongue swell, make me clumsy and slow. I seem to live behind a thick wall of cellophane. But the drugs helped me get words back. They come out very slowly now, but at least it's English.

Hirsch says that's progress. He says I'm making progress all the time. Opening my eyes, finding words — he says these are 'tremendous steps' in the right direction. He's pleased with me, I can tell. I am one of his successes. He thinks this is better. I don't. I would rather go back to being blind and crazy. At least then I didn't remember.

Hirsch comes to see me three times a week. I have a private room, very small but private. Sometimes he just sits, here at this chair at the desk. I sit on the daybed. Sometimes he talks to me. Sometimes, if I am able, I talk to him. He is a middle-aged man with black hair, but balding. He wears suits and ties; he is round in the middle and his shoulders stoop some. Hirsch is okay.

Besides me, he is taking care of my parents. It's been very hard having me in the hospital, especially on my mother. She feels so guilty, although none of it is her fault. Hirsch tells her that. She had nothing to do with it, nothing. But then she feels guilty about that, too. Hirsch told both my parents to leave me alone for now and I'm grateful for that. He's kept them off my back.

My mother came to the hospital one time after I opened my eyes and got down on her *knees* and started weeping, saying "What is it, Livvie? Tell me. What did I do wrong?" It was after that that Hirsch told them not to visit for a while. Mom thinks maybe I'm here because Dad was always getting transferred and we were constantly moving around, or maybe because I'm an only child, or because I had allergies, or because I was sick when I was a baby, or because she toilet trained me the wrong way. Or something. What she doesn't realise, cannot take in, is that I am in a mental institution because I choose to be, because it is the sanest place I have found in this world. And for now Hirsch lets me do what I want.

I suspect Hirsch got the idea for me to write this all down from my mother. When I was a little kid I used to say I wanted to be a writer when I grew up. I was always writing stories. I know she's told him. Actually, I also wanted to be a movie star and a figure skater but I doubt she mentioned that.

Hirsch has asked me to tell this story from beginning to end. Slowly. I would rather not. He is hopeful it will help me, although I know better. I can't be cured against my will. Perhaps when he has read this I'll be shipped off to State after all. I know he doesn't want to do that and I suppose it is good of him to care. But maybe not. Caring is what happened to me; it is how I came to be here.

But Hirsch, because you care I will tell it to you. Slowly. From beginning to end. Don't expect miracles.

0

THE BEGINNING

1

Funny, but it's not difficult to look back and say yes, this all began just then. Because there was a 'just then', a moment when it all began.

It was the first day of school, ninth grade. I walked into what was *supposed* to be Mrs. Fulton's biology class. I was lost or thought I was. The school was new to me; so was the town. We'd moved there just a few weeks before and I didn't know anybody. That day I was fourteen years old, and I had been the new kid in a new school six times already. Being lost was old. So was being new. I was looking down at my class card trying to match room numbers. One-twenty was the number, so this was the room. It was set up like a laboratory — beakers and plants and bones, microscopes and Bunsen burners sat on the counters that ringed the room. Instead of desks we had tables. It was a large, light room and I stood for a moment just inside the doorway taking my bearings.

And that's when I first saw David. He was grinning at me, sitting at the table closest to the door. His hair was wavy brown and he had big ears. That was my first thought about him — big ears, nice smile. He nodded at the chair across from him and I sat down.

"Hi," he said. "You look lost."

"I am, a little," I admitted.

"Bio 200, Mrs. Fulton," he said.

I consulted my card. "Uh huh."

"Well this is the place, and that's Mrs. Fulton." He nodded his head toward the woman standing at the front of the room.

She looked about forty, a trim woman with short blondish-grey hair. She was just standing at the front of the room near the chalkboard, gazing out the windows at the back. She wasn't trying to get our attention. She didn't even appear to be waiting for the class to get quiet the way some teachers do. She was simply standing there looking out the window. From time to time she'd rock back on her heels and frown a bit. It made wrinkles on her forehead.

I stacked my books in a neat pile and set them on the floor. I took out the new notebook that I'd already marked Biology and a pencil. I thought I was ready. Hah.

I have tried long and hard to blame Mrs. Fulton for what came later, but it doesn't work. She had something to do with it for sure, but what happened wasn't her fault. She was different, an eccentric, unlike any teacher I'd ever had before. It's easy to point to someone like that and say, "You're to blame." But it doesn't make it so.

That day, third period, even after the bell rang, Mrs. Fulton just stood there at the front of the room, looking. For the first few minutes people shifted around in their seats, talked, waved to old friends around the room.

"I'm David Kindler," David said to me.

"I'm Livvie Sinclair," I told him. And we both smiled. Just like that. After a while, it grew quiet in there. We were all waiting for Mrs. Fulton to do something.

"You know," she said slowly, as though she was in the middle of a conversation with someone we couldn't see, "I've been thinking."

David turned in his chair and caught my eye. "That's obvious," he whispered, grinning. I smiled back and shook my head slightly to indicate "Does this woman have all her marbles?"

"Later on in the year," Mrs. Fulton continued, "there's a unit in our book on human reproduction. That's all the sex education ninth graders are supposed to get."

Her comments were directed to the old gnarled oak tree just outside the window. I turned my head to look — several people did. It seemed there must be something out there, so intently was she looking. I would not have been surprised to see an angel perched in its branches, but there was only a tree. "Recently, just this summer in fact," she continued in this distant, far-away voice, "I had some experiences that made me think what sex education you kids get is too little too late."

I heard chairs squeak, papers shuffle. Someone dropped a book, a pencil. It rolled along the floor.

"I had a summer job at the health department down-town," she said. "Mostly what I did was analyse blood and urine samples."

"Oh gross," somebody giggled, and for the first time since class had started Mrs. Fulton lowered her gaze from the window and looked around the room. She smiled uncertainly, as though she were a little surprised to find herself standing in front of a classroom of students. "It doesn't sound too exciting, does it?" she asked. "Blood and urine. But you'd be surprised. At any rate, it was work. And money."

She brought her hands together in a cup and stared into them for a moment. Then briskly, decisively, she shook them out and brushed them on her skirt. "Besides that, I learned some things. There are hundreds of pregnant teenagers in this city. Hundreds."

I began to see where this was leading.

"Oh, I knew it up here," she said tapping herself on the forehead. Her voice was picking up strength. "I read the papers, I knew what the statistics said, but I never really knew. Not really."

She broke off and turned her gaze back to the window. When she looked at us again, she did it with such attention it made me squirm. A lot of other people seemed to have felt the same way. A general mutter rose in the room and a shifting of feet. She studied us face by face, slowly looking.

"So here's the point," she said finally, squinting up

her eyes as though to bring this point more closely into focus. "I'm going to spend the whole first semester, between now and Thanksgiving, on sex education. I'll cover everything in the book, plus anything else I can think of. And I expect you to help by asking questions so I know what it is you need to know."

The air in the room exploded. Somebody cheered, somebody whistled. A bunch of people groaned and some guys in the back started making fart noises, blowing air through their hands. Sex education. I sat very still staring at the empty sheet of paper in front of me. I darted one quick glance across the table at David. He sat sprawled in the chair facing Mrs. Fulton, legs out, arms folded across his chest, grinning at her like she'd just said something wonderful.

I want him to look at me like that, I thought suddenly, unexpectedly, with a heavy thump of my heart. He looked delighted with her. Without any warning I wanted him to look at *me* like that. I began to blush and looked down at my fingers, my pencil, my lap. I was sitting there blushing when Mrs. Fulton said, "I'm blushing."

I looked up at her then and sure enough she was turning an uncomfortable, dark shade of red. In the months that followed, I became so familiar with both David and Mrs. Fulton that their mannerisms became second nature to me. It's odd to remember discovering them, but I do.

Mrs. Fulton had the unusual habit of disclosing the moment. Soon I would be accustomed to hearing her say things like, "I'm blushing" or, "This makes me really uncomfortable" or, "I feel embarrassed." But at first, it was disconcerting. Most teachers don't tell you much about themselves. Mrs. Fulton didn't either, not normal stuff anyway. To this day I couldn't tell you much about her. Is she married? Divorced? Where does she live? I don't know. I know she has kids because she told us so once, and I know little odds and ends about her like she loves chocolate. But most of what I know is how she felt and thought, moment to moment, in sex-ed class, first semester.

Blushing, she went on to say how embarrassed she felt talking about sex. Hearing somebody tell you what she's feeling has the effect of making you aware of what *you're* feeling. Or at least it did with me.

She tried to get us to think about being embarrassed. Why was it hard to talk about sex? For her part she mentioned that her poor mother would turn in her grave if she knew her daughter was teaching sex education. I laughed thinking of Mrs. Fulton as somebody's daughter. She seemed so old. People raised their hands and called out other reasons like because there were both boys and girls in the class and because some people had had sex and some people hadn't. A tall girl at another table said, "Because it's private," and I thought, Amen.

"Yes," Mrs. Fulton agreed. "Our sexual feelings and our sexual behaviour are very private parts of who we are." She agreed, but it didn't stop her from talking about it.

That first day she said she knew perfectly well that some of us were already having sex and that some of us would have it soon no matter what. I sneaked a few glances around the room thinking, Who's having sex? How can you tell? Mrs. Fulton said she'd decided, after her summer at the health department, that she had a moral obligation to do something. And for her, that something was to teach sex education as openly and thoroughly as she could.

"I believe in education," she said. "And I believe, at least up here," she tapped her forehead again, "that information is protective. The more you know about something, the less vulnerable you are. But there's still so much I don't know about this. I've never taught sex-ed before except what's in the book, which is, I've begun to realise, a bit dated. I'm not sure how to go about this or whether it will do the least bit of good. But I am certain that I need to do *something*. This summer, those statistics I'd read about suddenly had names and faces attached to them. I'd see the girls come in, usually with a girlfriend, sometimes with a guy. They'd hand up their sample and I could see, in every one of them, how scared they were. It's a horrible thing to be fourteen and pregnant."

Mrs. Fulton sought the window and gazed at mid-distance for what seemed a long time. "It's not that great to be pregnant at any age if you didn't plan on it," she said at last, speaking to the tree outside. "But at fourteen, thirteen — we had an eleven-year old in there — it's worse." She shook her head.

Suddenly she became aware of the time. Our first class was almost over. She hadn't taken roll or handed out books or even told us her name. Most people knew who she was, but she'd never introduced herself or done any of the usual first day things.

"For homework tonight," she said and then waited until the boos died down, "think about what sex is."

"We will, we will," somebody called out.

She laughed. "I'm sure you will. Remember, I said *think*. This is not hands-on homework. We'll talk about it tomorrow."

We were dismissed. David swung back around in his seat and I got a good look at him. There were freckles on his nose; his face was wide and calm. He smiled, and I did too without even meaning to. I got out my class card and studied it to avoid staring at him.

"Where do you go next?" he asked me.

"Room 419," I told him. "Algebra. Ugh."

"I've got English." He looked at his card. "It's 303. Okay if I walk up with you?"

That's how it started between us. That's exactly how. I liked him and he liked me too. Right away. There wasn't any build up, it was just there between us. From the very, very start.

"This class is going to be wild," he said, gathering up his books and inclining his head towards Mrs. Fulton, who was now sitting at her desk, writing.

"She sure is . . ." I couldn't think of the right word. "Different." That was close enough.

"Yeah. I'm glad she's doing it, but I hope she

doesn't get in trouble," David said, falling into step with me. (That night at dinner when Mom asked me how school was I said, "Fine." "Any homework?" she said routinely. I thought of saying, "Yeah, I'm supposed to think about sex for Mrs. Fulton's class." I could imagine Mom choking on her broccoli, could picture my dad's eyebrows shooting up. The image made me smile but I realised then exactly what David had meant about Mrs. Fulton getting into trouble. Instead, I told Mom I had a dumb story to read for English and a little algebra.)

The halls in that school are crowded. How nice to walk next to someone so tall! And David was tall — thin and tall. His blue-jeaned legs were so long! Even though he was a freshman there too, he seemed to know his way around. When we got up to the third floor landing, we said goodbye. And as I was swept away down the hall by the crowd I heard him yell, "See you tomorrow, Livvie Sinclair." He remembered my name.

I hadn't planned on finding David my first day at school. I certainly hadn't planned on liking him or having him like me. The only boys I'd known before were so immature that I thought they were stupid. It's not nice to say, but it's the truth. Back in the sixth and seventh grades, girls were falling in love all over the place. Almost everybody I knew had a crush (or worse) on someone and I never understood it. I assumed that someday, when I was older, much older, I'd meet a *man* and maybe fall in love. I never imagined there could be a boy like David in the ninth grade. But he was.

2

The next day David tapped me on the shoulder just outside of class. He was smiling like he was glad to see me. I felt the same. "Livvie," he said. "Is that short for Olivia?"

"'Fraid so."

"Livvie," he said again. "It's got a nice sound to it. I like it." I couldn't think of anything to say. He liked my name. I liked his too.

We sat down at the same table as yesterday. Kids were coming in, and Mrs. Fulton wasn't there yet.

"Did you do your homework?" a girl with three-colour hair asked David as she joined us at the table. This was Helen. We were in two classes together besides this one and she was impossible not to know. She wore huge, bangly jewellery and clanged everywhere she went.

"Yeah, I did," David told her, grinning. "Did you?" He asked Helen but he included me with his eyes, which were smiling brown and crinkled at the edges. I have yet to see the like.

"You better believe it." Helen laughed, falling back in her chair in a mock swoon. "Think about sex. I haven't done my homework so well since I was in the second grade. Unnhh. Job well done."

I had to laugh. After I got to know Helen a little, I laughed at her a lot. She wanted it. We weren't friends exactly but I liked her. She was sort of a loudmouth, but more a clown than a troublemaker. I wouldn't want to be her, but I admired her guts. I've always been kind of quiet, and Helen is the direct opposite.

Moving around every two or three years is not as bad as people imagine. One of the benefits is that there is always a chance to start over. (I have always needed all the chances at this I could get.) Every time we moved, I made resolutions about how I was going to change and be a different, better person. This time, one of my goals was to be more outspoken. Not as much as Helen, but more so than I had been, which was almost not at all.

"I thought about it too," David told Helen. "What is sex?" He smiled at her. "Until I started thinking about it, I thought I knew."

"You mean you don't know?" Helen teased him. "Maybe I could explain it to you sometime." She was batting her eyes at him, but not really flirting.

Mrs. Fulton came in just then and we all turned to look at her.

"Well? Have you thought about sex?" she asked.

"I fucking well did," somebody in the back yelled out. A lot of people giggled nervously. I, for one. Mrs. Fulton looked at him. (I don't know this guy's name.

He cut class a lot, but when he was there he yelled out stuff like that all the time.)

"Okay," Mrs. Fulton said calmly, "fucking is certainly part of it. Now, just so we're all talking about the same thing, would you explain it?" I was shocked. I'd never heard a teacher use that word and for a moment I couldn't breathe.

"Screwing."

"Well, screwing and fucking are slang words for the same thing," she answered.

"I know some other words for it," he said.

"I'll bet you do," she laughed. "There are hundreds of slang words for sexual intercourse. I suppose it's some kind of measurement of our embarrassment about it, as a society. How many slang terms are there for elbow, for instance? Hardly anybody's embarrassed about elbows, so we just call them that and have done with it." She paused and looked around the room. "Is sex anything else besides a man's penis going into a woman's vagina?"

I felt a surge of blood rush into my face when she said those words. Somehow the real names of things about sex are much more embarrassing for me than the slang. Vagina sounds yucky, and penis, I don't know, it seems weird.

Helen said sex had to do with love. Mrs. Fulton nodded.

"It does if you're lucky," she said. "But people can have sex without being in love, and they can love each other a lot and not have sex."

"What's the point of that?" someone asked.

"What do you mean?"

"I mean if you love somebody, why *not* have sex? It seems like a waste not to."

"Well, maybe it's not what's best for them just then. You can't prove you love somebody by having sex with them. Whatever sex is, it isn't a proof of anything. That much I'm sure of."

David said, "I think it's mostly in the joining, the mixing. It's the blending of two people."

Mrs. Fulton gave him a smile. "I think you're right."

"You make it sound like a recipe instruction," Helen muttered at him under her breath. David grinned at her.

"That's sort of how I think of it," he whispered back.

I was wondering how he knew so much.

"Sex is a joining," Mrs. Fulton was saying. "Part of it is the physical, but it can also be a coming together of spirits."

As soon as she said the word spirits, people started laughing and somebody hummed the theme music from "The Twilight Zone". Uuuoooouuuooo. She laughed. "I suppose spirits is a pretty big word. But I can't think of anything smaller for what I'm trying to say. You can have sexual intercourse on just the physical level, but that isn't going all the way. All the way involves the whole person, including that awkward part of them I'm calling the spirit. You all are how old in here? — fourteen? fifteen? That's too young to have sex, too young to mingle that intimately with another person. I don't want you to."

"This is nothing but the same old line with some bull about spirits thrown in. You're too young." It was the guy in the back. "I'm sick of hearing it. How old do you think we have to be?"

"I'm not sure," Mrs. Fulton said quietly. "I know just getting older doesn't guarantee that a person gets ready for sex. I'm not saying you have simply to reach a certain birthday and then it's okay. It doesn't work like that. I think that before you can get that close, really get that close, you need to develop yourself."

"So I'm developed," he said. "And I can assure you my girlfriend is." He put his hands out to show she had big breasts. There was a lot of snickering.

Mrs. Fulton squinted her eyes and didn't say anything. She was frowning, but she didn't look mad. Finally she shook her head. "No, there's more to it. If your goal is to create a loving relationship that lasts for a long time, maybe your life, then you need to take your time developing it. It's like building a house. If you want it to be strong, you need to spend some time on the foundation. Part of it is self-awareness, part of it is caring. If you become aware of who you are and learn to care about yourself, you will be able, in time, to know and care for someone else."

"I never thought sex could be so boring," Helen said, just loud enough for Mrs. Fulton to hear. She turned and smiled at her. Helen and David and I were the only ones sitting at that table. I felt my cheeks burning.

"Oh, it's not all that boring. Take tonight's homework. In fact, it's your homework for the next week: I want you each to stand, in private, in front of a mirror fully naked and look at yourself. While you're looking, I want you to say, 'I am a beautiful and valuable person.' Say it several times. You're not allowed to criticise what you see. If you're used to saying that you hate your thighs and think they're too fat, you have to banish that thought from your mind while you're doing this assignment. You're just supposed to look and say that you're beautiful and valuable. Five minutes a night for a week. Any questions?" Nobody raised a hand, but a lot of people talked.

"Are you serious?"

"I am."

"This is totally gross."

"No it's not."

"What is the point? I mean why?"

"Well, I want you to get to know yourself. That's what the looking is for, and I want you to be kind to yourself. That's why the words."

"Do we get graded on this? I mean how will you know if we do it?"

"I won't. And no, there's no grade for it. I want you to do it. I wouldn't ask you to if I didn't think it was important. It is important."

"Have you ever done it?"

"Yes."

a few minutes, there were no more questions. I ...dn't imagine doing it, but I thought I might try. The night before, when we were supposed to be thinking about what sex is, I kept blanking out. It was like an old-fashioned movie or TV show where the camera fades out right after the kiss. I couldn't get it to go any further.

"There's another project in here that you won't be graded on," Mrs. Fulton continued. "I hope you don't just work for grades, because if you do, you won't get too much out of this. Between now and Thanksgiving, which is the end of the first term, I want you to care about someone. You can have this first week, while you're doing the mirror exercise, to think about it. I'd like you to choose someone you never thought much of caring about in the first place. Surprise yourself. A week from today, which will be — " she looked down at the calender on her desk — "September fourth, I want you to hand in a paper telling me who the person is."

She paused and looked out the window a while. "Sex has to do with caring. I don't want you to have sex while you're in the ninth grade. I've said that, and I mean it. But one day, I want you to be able to be close, very close, to another human being. Think of this as practice if you want or think of it as homework. However you think of it, do it."

"Are we supposed to *do* anything about this person, besides care?" somebody asked.

"Well, sure. In fact, the easiest way to start caring about someone is to do something. Think about the person, think of something you could do that would be appreciated, and do it. Then think of something else and do that."

"Is it supposed to be a secret?"

"Well, no, not exactly. You can talk it over with one or two other people, but don't go bragging it up. I don't suggest telling the person 'Hey, you're my term project for science.' That might get taken the wrong way."

"Can this be anyone?"

"Yes."

"I can think of somebody who would appreciate it if I'd have sex with him," Helen said. Everybody laughed. "Well, I can," she persisted. "I mean he really wants to."

"No. I don't want you to use sex to show you care," Mrs. Fulton said. "Find another way or find another person if he hassles you too much. Remember, we're working in here on the foundation. Don't jump ahead. It's hard to backtrack."

Helen shook her head. "I don't get it."

"That's okay for right now. You don't have to understand it to fulfil the assignment."

She spent the rest of the period talking about why she thought teenagers shouldn't have sex. She could get really old on this subject. Her first point was that she didn't think we were 'emotionally mature enough' to handle that much intimacy. Personally, I didn't think this was any of her business. The second point was that teenagers tend to use birth control unreliably. Statistics show — something or other. I have a bad habit of tuning out immediately after the word 'statistics'. This could be because my dad is a statistician, but I'm not sure. I just don't hear anything after that word.

When she got excited — and Mrs. Fulton could get very excited — she bounded up and down on her toes. When she was really going full steam she walked around the room gesturing with her hands, drawing pictures in the air. (Actually, the air pictures were a relief after seeing what she was capable of with a piece of chalk. I remember that day she was trying to explain how a girl could still get pregnant even if she was having her period. She drew a picture of what she *said* was a uterus on the board and then she attached the fallopian tubes and the ovaries. It looked exactly like a Martian with little antennae waving around. She looked at the picture for a minute and then groaned and erased it. "I'm a terrible artist," she explained unnecessarily and then continued talking, walking around the tables.)

Her nose was very long and she had a thin pointy chin, which makes her sound like a witch and she wasn't that. Her eyes were real, real green. (I always suspected tinted contacts.) When she was trying to think of how to explain something she would squint her eyes and that squint would make her nose look even longer. She wasn't pretty but there was something about her that made her easy to get used to.

That day, and many days thereafter, I got the distinct impression that Mrs. Fulton didn't really need us. Don't get me wrong, she cared — a lot — about sex education, but she wasn't desperate about it. She wanted this class, this approach to make a difference with us, but she didn't agonise over it. Despite all her blushing and fumbling around for the right word I think she was having a good time. She was like a scientist trying our a new hypothesis, which is, I guess, exactly what she was.

When the bell finally rang, David turned around in his chair and caught my eye. "I think I really like this lady," he said.

"I think I do too," I answered truthfully, "but some of it's making me real nervous. You know?" Saying 'you know?' after every sentence was one of the bad habits I'd been trying to change. I wasn't getting too far with it.

"Yeah, I do know," he said, smiling. "This is a first. Maybe high school isn't going to be so bad."

"Well, what about this homework?" Helen asked. "Have you ever? Think about what sex is. Look at yourself in the mirror, care about someone else. Jeez. I can't figure her out. What does any of it have to do with sex?"

"Are you going to do it?" David asked.

She looked at him a long time. "Yeah, I think I am," she said at last in a slightly different tone. "Why not? It's nutty, but I think I'll give it a try. I kind of like her too. How do you think she grades in here?"

"If we don't get pregnant between now and Thanksgiving it's an automatic A," I said. They both laughed. I was blushing again. I'm pretty fair-skinned so it really shows.

"Well, *he* won't have anything to worry about then," Helen said, indicating David.

"Maybe the guys have to sign a pledge," David said. "You know, I promise not to have sex until I really care about myself and somebody else, and to use a rubber when I do." I was suddenly aware that David was blushing too.

Helen snorted. "You're a hoot. See you guys later."

Classes were changing. I had algebra to get to; David had English. "Listen," he said as we walked out together, "would it be okay if I called you sometime?" I nodded yes. Okay? It would be great. I didn't say it, but I think he saw it on my face. "So what's your number?" I told him. He didn't write it down, but he listened so closely that I knew he'd memorised it. "Livvie," he said as I turned to go up to the fourth floor, "I'm really glad we're in class together. I mean it."

"I am too," I said, blushing again. He smiled.

"So do you take the bus or what?"

"No, I live just a couple of blocks from here. Over in the High Ridge subdivision," I told him.

"No kidding? I live over there too. I could walk home with you. You want to meet after school?"

Yes. Somehow I managed to tell him yes and we arranged the place to meet. By the flagpole. And that afternoon he walked me home.

3

To get home from school we had to walk only a few blocks to the highway and across this covered walkway that goes above the road. Our subdivision spreads out over a hill that used to be a cow pasture. There's still a creek of sorts running along one edge of it. Mostly though it's split-level ranch houses and fake colonials, sidewalks, green lawns, and driveways. David and his mother lived in a house on Ashwood. I lived just seven blocks away. Bayberry Court. (Part of what makes it so hard now is this sense that he and I were meant to be. There were so many little things we had in common. It seemed fated somehow that out of all the people, all the chances we had of meeting, we did meet. We did.)

David and I were both walkers. That in itself is kind of unusual. We liked walking. We both preferred not to ask our parents to drive us places. In the suburbs it's a whole lot faster to drive, but David and I had each figured out independently that you could get away more easily with less hassle if you walked. By ourselves we had come to that same conclusion. Doesn't that count for something? Our families were so different, but David and I were not. Somehow we were not.

My parents are almost entirely, I'd say religiously, conventional. David's mother, Marie, on the other hand, is decidedly unusual.

My father, as I've said, is a statistician. He works for IBM. In the last twelve years we've lived in six different cities; we're good at moving. IBM demands it. My mother sells Avon. She says it's good for her because she can do it anywhere we live, and I can see her point. Actually, it's inaccurate to say we've lived in six different cities; we've lived in the suburbs of six different cities. For all our moving around, it hasn't been that big of an adjustment in any one place. Suburbs must look alike everywhere. At least from what I've seen.

I guess I grew up always knowing I'd be leaving soon. I've had friends, I've always had friends, but nobody very close. We'd move and none of us ever did much about keeping in touch. Sometimes a letter or a Christmas card, but usually not. I learned to leave people behind, say goodbye, get going. Most of the things I like to do, reading and writing and cooking and walking, I can do by myself. I never went out for team sports or cheerleading or band or drama. My hobbies were solitary and portable.

David meanwhile had lived in High Ridge almost his entire life. He was friends with people he'd known from back in kindergarten. Helen, for instance. Lots of people. He and Helen told me a story about what they'd done one time to torture a math substitute back in sixth grade. Helen, who doesn't wear them, pretended she'd lost a contact lens. The whole class got down on their hands and knees and crawled around on the floor pretending to look for it. They kept it up until the bell rang and then she hollered, "Found it!" and everyone got up and left. They could look back and remember things together. I kind of envied that at first.

It seemed to me that everyone liked David, everyone knew him. They did. He'd never once been the new kid, never once had to explain himself to anyone. Everyone already knew — that's David Kindler. Period. But for all that difference in our backgrounds and our experiences, we were just the same inside. For all his friends, there was nobody that really knew David. Not really. Until me. Me he let in.

We met by the flagpole and David walked me home that day. He asked about my family and told me he was an only child too, that he lived with his mother. I assumed (wrongly) that his parents were divorced. Somewhat unwillingly — he wanted to meet her — I introduced him to my mother. Mom gave David the once over and decided he was okay. I could almost see her ticking off her list: nice looking boy, good manners, doesn't appear to do drugs, doesn't drive a motorcycle — these were the main points of her concern. (She is absolutely hyper about boys on motorcycles.) Later, she made it a point to sell Marie some Avon and take a look at their house. After that she left us alone. Which was exactly what I wanted.

I know Mom blames herself now, wonders what she should have, could have done, but there is nothing. If she and Dad knew David the way I did they would understand better, now, how I feel. But I didn't want them to. I kept him to myself.

4

My parents didn't get to know the Parkers either. Nobody paid them much attention except for David and me and that was fine with us. Stupid us. Actually, everybody on Bayberry Court paid them a lot of attention the day they moved in — it was impossible not to — but after that David and I were the only ones.

It was Labour Day weekend, a week after school started, the first Saturday in September, when Dean and Maggie Parker drove down Bayberry Court in a U-Haul truck. They pulled in at the very bottom of the street, where it dead ends at the steps leading up to the Emsley Place.

Back when this was a farm, the Emsley Place was the farm house. It sits up on the ridge that the subdivision is named for, looking totally out of place, even though it was here first. It's a big, white house with a flapping shingle roof and a wide, high, sloping, green porch. Above it is a tangled old apple orchard, completely gone to brambles, and then off above that is where the highway cuts through. People whizzing by in their cars can look down and see it. Beneath it the tidy houses of High Ridge spread out like a fan. Our house is the next to last at the end of Bayberry. That's where the steps are, leading up to the Emsley Place.

When we first moved there, the little kid next door told me the place was haunted. He was joking but only a little. Old man Emsley had died in there seven years before, and nobody had lived there since. At least until the Parkers. The house *looks* haunted. Maybe it is. If not before, perhaps now. The foundation is cracked, the paint has chipped off, and the shutters hang crooked. If they leave it alone, the whole place will collapse, cave in on itself and succumb to its wounds. For now it still stands, the wind moaning in its chimneys. What will probably happen is that the neighbourhood association will declare it unsightly, unworthy of High Ridge, and it will be destroyed. Do I care?

The Parkers pulled in at the very bottom of the hill. The only way up is the steps, two and a half steep, cracked concrete flights of them. Mrs. Parker got out of the truck, looked up at the house, back at her husband and collapsed in the street. I didn't see it, but I heard voices raised and came out on the lawn to see what was going on. Mom did too. So did just about everybody else on the street.

A lot of people were flapping around her, talking at once. Just then David came up beside me. I guess you could say it was our first date. We'd arranged to meet and take a walk together. He came up so quietly (and I was watching the hubbub around Mrs. Parker so intently) that I hadn't heard him. "Can we use your phone?" he asked, real low.

I was startled at first, and then flushed with the closeness of him, but I nodded yes and we went into my house, straight into the kitchen, where he dialled the emergency number. My dad wasn't home and Mom was out with the other women bent over Mrs. Parker. When we came back out Mrs. Parker was coming to. I saw her blinking.

David put his hand on the back of my neck and gave a little squeeze. "You okay?" he asked me.

"Yeah," I told him and smiled. I liked the way he had simply appeared, the way he had called the ambulance like he knew what he was doing, the way he touched my neck and asked how I was. We both just stood there watching.

When Mrs. Parker came all the way to, she tried to sit up. She put her hands up to her face, then slumped back down. I think she was crying. Mr. Parker was standing up, looking down at her, glancing over at the rest of us who were either hovering near or standing on our lawns and in our driveways, watching. Finally the ambulance came. The medics put her on a stretcher and lifted her into the van. Mr. Parker climbed in too.

When the ambulance pulled away everyone stood around looking at each other. Mom was out meeting her neighbours. We'd moved there ourselves only a month before and there were plenty of people I saw that day whom I've never seen since. This is not a neighbourhood where people sit out in their front yards. So in a way it was surprising when someone, I forget who, got the idea to unpack the U-Haul for the Parkers. The truck, of course, was still sitting there; the keys were still in the ignition.

I helped. David helped. We all did. It was like a block party. We carried up lamps and chairs, a blue plaid sofa, a TV, a thousand and four boxes of I don't know what — clothes, pots and pans, dishes, papers, books, stuff. We carried up a big mattress and a box spring, the headboard, dressers, tables, and a crib. The crib made everyone talk. Was she expecting? Is that why she fainted?

The women mostly stayed up in the house and arranged the furniture as best they could. Some went home and came back with casseroles, soft drinks, beer. The men puffed it out on the steep, uneven steps that led up to the house. It was fun. Even now, when I know what came of it all, I can't in good faith say any different. At the time, there was a mood of celebration. People were laughing. It was strange and fun to be doing something all together, as neighbours. I was full, too, of David and the fun of working with him, of being partners with him.

At about five o'clock, Mr. Parker came back. He arrived in a cab. He was a big burly man dressed in work clothes, not a suit. His face looked grey and set with fatigue. David and I were just unloading a bookcase together, laughing at each other and threatening to drop it when the cab pulled up. Mr. Parker stared at us and we both quieted down immediately. He looked furious.

David said, "Here, Livvie, set it down," and I did. He dusted his hands off on his jeans and walked down the steps to where Mr. Parker was. "Hello, sir," he said, holding out his hand. "I'm David Kindler. We thought we'd get you all moved in. How's your wife?" God. He was polite as hell.

Mr. Parker grunted. He neither shook David's hand nor answered him. He stared at him a moment, stared at me, and climbed the steps, two at a time. David bit his bottom lip. I felt bad for him — David with his perfect manners, his good intentions. Even then it didn't occur to us that our help wasn't necessarily wanted. I remember thinking briefly, What if they aren't going to stay? The truck was almost unloaded by then.

David and I followed him up the stairs, bookcase between us. We set it down in the living room, up against a still empty wall and walked into the front hall. From there we could see Mr. Parker shaking hands with the men in the kitchen. We heard him say that 'the little lady was in the family way' and that the doctor thought she would be all right after a while. The strain of moving. He thanked everyone and took a beer. David motioned to me with his head toward the front door and we left. We skipped down the steps and were gone.

David was the taller one, but our step always matched when we walked. Partly it's because I'm mostly legs, but also I keep thinking it has to do with how right we were with each other. That afternoon, it felt good to get out of there, to quit working, to be by ourselves. He showed me a place he liked to walk to, an undeveloped tract of land down near the creek. If you cross the creek there — and it's easy to do if you jump rocks — it's a shortcut to the mall. People in cars never know these things. We walked by his house and he pointed it out to me, but I didn't meet Marie until later.

That day, I remember, we held hands for the first time. I was glad, deeply glad when he reached over and caught my hand, but I was also something I never would have expected — comfortable. We talked. We goofed around. He was so easy to be with.

We had an idea to make the Parkers our sex-ed caring project. Which one of us thought of it first? I wish I could remember. Not that it matters anymore. It may be that like a lot of things between us, it came to us both at the same time. It seemed perfect. We assumed they needed caring about. It wasn't every day that someone collapsed on the street in Bayberry Court. And they satisfied the requirement that they be someone we had never thought of caring for before. We'd never even met them.

"I wonder if Mrs. Fulton would let us," I said. "You know, do it together."

"Why not? If we teamed up we could be more help."

"You're right. That place is so run down. The

kitchen floor has tar on it or something. We could scrub it."

"Yeah, and that lawn is going to be a true pain in the neck to mow. It's practically straight up and down. With two of us working..."

"Well, it makes sense. I mean there are two of them and two of us. It's a great idea. If she'll let us."

"She didn't say everyone *had* to work alone, did she?"

"No, I don't think so. And in a case like this, where there's so much to do. I mean why not? It seems logical."

"I think I can stop that drip in their sink," David said.

"You know how to do that?" I was impressed.

"Yeah." I noticed that he suddenly looked a little shy. He ran both his hands through his hair, ruffling it. "I know how to do lots of stuff around a house."

"Well, I was thinking I could take her some brownies. I'm really good on brownies."

"Oh you are, are you?" I could hear the teasing in his voice, the smile. "Maybe you need an impartial opinion on that before you go spreading them around the neighbourhood. After all, you wouldn't want to make 'the little lady' sicker than she already is."

"David Kindler! You skunk!" I reached over to poke him in the ribs but he caught my hand and then caught the other. He held me there, shaking his head while I made faces at him, both of us laughing.

We walked another hour in the gathering dusk,

making plans, telling jokes, holding hands. We were full of ideas, of hope. Back then, we thought caring was defined by what you did. And we were willing to do plenty.

5

Mrs. Fulton didn't mind. We handed in a paper describing what little we knew of the Parkers and what we planned to do for them — together. She read it, looked us both over, and with a grin, nodded fine. "If nothing else, you'll learn something about working together. If you can stand it."

We could stand it, all right. Within that first week we established the pattern that was ours from then on — we spent our free time together, as much as was possible. Almost immediately people recognised us as a couple and I was quickly, effortlessly, a somebody by sheer association. I overheard two girls in the bathroom at school. I had shut the door to the stall when one of them asked the other who I was. "She's David Kindler's girl." The sound of it swept through me, leaving me tingly with pride.

I imagine a baby who takes its first steps experiences something similar. The walking is new and thrilling, and yet it feels completely right. It's been in the baby's bones since birth. Being with David must have been born in my bones. When it happened, I knew I had been waiting for it all my life.

Mrs. Fulton asked the whole class one day if we'd been doing our mirror assignments. Nobody said a word and she changed the subject saying only, "I hope so." I'd been doing it as best I could, but it was impossible for me to look in the mirror and not criticise what I saw.

I have frizzy blonde hair that's hard to brush. It's not soft or manageable or any of the other things hair is supposed to be. It's fairly long except for these totally goofy bangs on my forehead. I mean they don't lie down; they're springy. I've thought about cutting my hair but if I do, it might all be like my bangs — goofy. My skin is real pale. I've had a few zits but nothing serious. My eyes are grey. I really like looking at people's eyes; I do think you can tell a lot about them that way. My own eyes, though, don't tell me much. David used to say they told him plenty, that he could read my feelings by looking in them, but I don't see how. My nose is so-so; I've seen worse. But the part of my face I dislike the most is my mouth. I have fat lips. Okay, so that's criticism, but it's also the truth. There's a movie star who has fat lips, but on her it looks sexy. On me it looks ugly.

Looking at my face was the easy part. I'd never really looked at the rest of my body naked before. I mean, I'd looked at myself but not altogether, standing there, going over it. I'm real bony. My collarbones stick out a mile, and then there are my breasts. One is bigger than the other. Mrs. Fulton said that most people's are, especially during adolescence, and mine are like that. It's not a drastic difference, but one side — the right — is definitely bigger than the left. My breasts aren't huge but they're noticeable. I do tend to slump my shoulders to cover them up, which used to drive Mom nuts. "Stand up straight. Being a woman is nothing to be ashamed of." The nipples on my breasts are dark brown and they feel like chicken skin. Well, sometimes they do. They stick out, my nipples do, even when I wear a bra, which is usually. It's pretty bad. I tried wearing Band-Aids over them one time, but I kept thinking, What if I ended up in the emergency room somewhere and they undressed me and found Band-Aids on my nipples. That would be worse. So I discovered fuzzy sweaters, which hide them pretty well.

I have no waist to speak of; I mean it doesn't go in at all. Just straight down from my chest. My hipbones are pretty much like my collarbones, they jut. What's worse is that there's this pad of fat on my lower abdomen. It's not gross exactly, but it's definitely fat. Mrs. Fulton said that all girls and women have it. It's there to protect their uterus and ovaries. She said even girls who starve themselves — if they have anorexia, for instance — end up looking like skeletons except for that little pad of fat. It's nature's way of protecting our reproductive organs. Personally, I think nature could come up with something a little more attractive.

One very strange thing about my body is that my

pubic hair is darker than the hair on my head. It's brown and kind of crinkly. I'm not crazy about it, but it's also the hardest part of my body to look at. By the time I would get to 'down there' I would be rushing anyway. My thighs are fat. I don't know why, since I'm a basically skinny person, but they are. Fat. My knees are a crisscross of old scars. When I was little I used to get stitches in my knees on an average of once a month. The rest of my legs are just there, but I have really ugly feet. There's no way I can call them anything else. If I'm a beautiful and valuable person it's only on a long shot and only when I have shoes on.

Well, I did what Mrs. Fulton told us to. I looked, I tried, really not to be critical, and I repeated those words. Every night for a week. It was hard but I did it.

Walking home one afternoon, David brought it up. "Did you do the mirror exercise?" he asked.

"Yeah, I did it. But I didn't enjoy it. It felt really weird," I told him.

"I know. It was for me too," he said. "I don't like the way I look."

This took me by surprise. "Well, I like the way you look."

He started smiling and put his arm around my shoulder.

"Thanks, Livvie," he said softly. We just walked like that for a while, feeling it. "It was a strange assignment, wasn't it?"

"It was. That whole class is so different, David. One thing I'm having trouble with is that she's really not grading us. I mean, I've always complained about grades, how dumb they are and all that, but this is the first time I haven't even been able to work for one. You know?"

"I do. But on the other hand — " David did what he almost always did before he said something funny; he cocked his head and looked at me slanty-eyed, smiling — "if she's going to give homework like this, I'm glad she realises she can't check up on us."

I started laughing. "At least she knows her limits."

"You're right, though; it's odd to be doing something like that when it would be just as easy to lie and say you did it and not do it."

As part of her 'experiment' in first term Biology/Life Science, Mrs. Fulton had informed us that we all had an automatic A as long as we 1) showed up for class and 2) did the assignments. And the assignments were always things like Think about Sex, Look at Yourself in the Mirror, Imagine Yourself Grown-up, Think of Ten Things You Like About Yourself, and of course the term project — Care About Someone. Anybody could say they did it and get away with it; practically half the class did just that. But she kept her word. Kids who had never gotten an A their whole lives got A's that term in Biology.

I still do not understand why Mrs. Fulton set herself up to be taken advantage of. She's no dummy, and I suspect she had her reasons. But it was like she really didn't care if we tricked her or not. She told us early on that we would only be cheating ourselves. Teachers always say that, but then they still make you separate your desks and cover your paper. Mrs. Fulton made no effort to keep us from lying. She really believed her own line.

She gave us quizzes all the time, but she said — and it proved to be completely true — that they were only for her own use. She wanted to see how well we were picking up the information, but they would in no way affect our grade. (I flunked the first vocabulary quiz. Completely. I blanked out. It was a matching test and suddenly none of the words seemed connected to anything I knew about. I'd heard her say the words: vulva, labia, fallopian tubes, testicles, epididymis, penis, Cowper's gland, how many others? But seeing them in print was such a shock that I just forgot everything. It was embarrassing, but she never said anything about it. When she handed it back to me it was corrected, that's all. No grade.)

David and I considered ourselves (and each other) smarter than the average person. Maybe it doesn't sound very nice to say, but it's true. We never bragged about it, but we'd both always gotten good grades in elementary school and we knew how to do school. It had never been too hard for either one of us, but it wasn't a snap either. We weren't geniuses; we were good students. In a way, I think having an automatic A was harder on people like us, who were used to getting A's we'd worked for, than it was on people who worked and usually got B's or C's, or even on those who never worked at all but always got A's or F's.

But we adjusted. We had no intention of not doing the project we'd set up for ourselves. Our plan to help the Parkers wasn't dependent on a grade. It grew on its own, fuelled by how much fun it was to plan it, to talk about it with each other. In fact, we'd planned it so well and imagined so much that by the time Mrs. Parker came home from the hospital that next Friday, it took us a while to see that the first step might be harder than we'd anticipated.

6

The day she came home was my fifteenth birthday, September eighth. Personally, I don't get into my birthday too much. If I could I'd ignore it, but Mom likes to make a big deal of it. Since we'd just moved into the neighbourhood, she didn't push too hard when I said I didn't want a party. She did ask if I wanted to invite David over for dinner, but I didn't. I wasn't ashamed of my parents, exactly, I just couldn't see sitting around with David there listening to Dad say, "My little girl, growing up so fast." Plus — and this has happened more times than I can count — Mom gets off on her memories of the day I was born. It's embarrassing. So I hadn't even told David it was my birthday. I didn't want him to feel like he had to give me a present, and also, I just wanted to get it over with and *be* fifteen.

So I was more than a little dismayed when he knocked on the door in the middle of dinner.

"Why, David," I heard Mom say when she opened the door. "You're just in time for a piece of Livvie's birthday cake. What a pleasant surprise."

He came into the dining room looking sheepish. "I didn't know it was your birthday," he said. "I'm sorry to interrupt."

"You're not interrupting," Mom said. "Now it's more like a party."

"Hi," I said, feeling somehow caught in the act. "Have you eaten?"

"Yes." He sat down next to me. It's really strange that there are only three people in our family and our table can easily sit six or eight. Mom sits at one end, Dad at the other, and I sit in the middle. It's always been that way. David leaned over and whispered in my ear, very quickly, "There's something I've got to show you."

I raised my eyebrows at him to sign, What? But he mouthed, "Later," at me and turned to talk to my Dad. David was taking a computer class at school, and he and Dad had already had one conversation the week before, the first time they met, about some new line of software IBM was putting out. He actually liked my parents, especially my dad. He didn't have a father of his own, and I guess he wondered what it would be like.

The rest of dinner followed exactly the line of my worst fears. Mom brought out this big cake with fifteen candles on it and they all sang "Happy Birthday" to me with the lights out.

"Make a wish," Mom sing-songed as though I were three years old, and just as I was taking a breath to blow, David caught my eye and *winked* at me. That made me splutter and it took me two tries to get all the candles out. "It'll be two years before you get your wish," Dad chuckled as he turned the lights back on. And then, true to form, he sighed and said, "My little girl, growing up so fast." And Mom, who was still standing up, put her arm around my waist — I have been taller than her since I was twelve — and said, "You were such a little peanut of a thing when you were born." To David, by way of explanation, she launched into the whole story of how premature I was and how they'd had me in Intensive Care for three weeks and on and on. David actually winced when she said the part about how many needles were in my veins. He looked at me then with something so like sorrow on his face that I felt a wild leaping in my chest.

Most of the presents were okay. Mom and Dad gave me a gift certificate to a record shop in the mall, and a stereo cassette player of my own. Finally. And my grandmother sent me a string of pearls that were just beautiful. They had been hers when she was fifteen. But then Mom, wanting to do something 'personal', gave me a lacy white nightgown. As soon as I opened the box and felt the material, which was silky and smooth, I started blushing. If it sounds like I blushed a lot back then, it's true. I did. I held up the nightgown and thanked Mom, but the whole time I was trying not to look at David, who was looking at me with a kind of astonishment on his face I found painful and thrilling simultaneously.

We were finally able to leave. David told my parents

that since he hadn't known it was my birthday, he was going to take me out to look at the full moon as my present. "Well, be careful and have a good time," Mom said. She said that to me every time I went anywhere, no matter what. Outside, the moon was full, hugely so. It hung white and heavy in the sky. Although it would get unbearably hot again for a few weeks of Indian summer, that night there was a cool, faintly crisp breeze.

"So what's up?" I asked as soon as the door shut behind us and we were down the front walk.

"Come with me," he said and linked his arm in mine. I could feel his excitement. We walked to the bottom of the street to where the steps led up to the Parkers'. There, on one side at the bottom, was a large orange and black NO TRESPASSING sign.

"Oh-oh," I said. "What does it mean?"

"Just wait," David whispered and, climbing the hill away from the steps, he motioned me first to follow and then to get down.

"Where are we going?" I whispered back when I caught up to him. We were crouching in a stand of trees about halfway up the hill to the house. We could see the front porch from there and he pointed.

It took me a second to focus but then I saw it, hanging from the doorway — Do Not Disturb. The porch light was on and for a moment the house looked so ominous and forbidding that I felt a chill. 'What are we going to do?" I asked him. He shook his head.

"She's home, you know," he whispered.

"How do you know?"

"You're going to have to be really quiet. Okay?"

We climbed farther up the hill, keeping always in the trees, until we were actually just behind the house, behind their decrepit old toolshed, hidden in the apple orchard. Looking down, we could see plainly into their kitchen and into the bedroom directly above it. Mrs. Parker was reading in bed. The shades weren't drawn, and we could see her propped up against the pillows with her knees up under a quilt. Ringlets of thick, dark hair framed a pale face. I couldn't see much else from that distance. David and I didn't talk, we just watched. It was a weird thing to do, and I finally tugged on his sleeve and motioned that I was heading back down. This time, he followed me.

Outside the shed I stepped accidentally on a rake which then clattered against an old bucket. We both dove down and froze, waiting. Mr. Parker turned on the side light and opened the door that led from their kitchen. We were not ten yards from him, and I was sure the thumping of my heart would give us away. He stood looking out toward us, frowning, but it was dark by then and somehow we got away with it. When he went back inside we waited, heads pressed down into the cool grass. I counted to sixty as slowly as I could and then moved on down the rest of the hill, back to the sidewalk, back to the street. We turned up Bayberry and kept walking, neither one of us saying a word until we were out of the court and around the corner.

"David, I don't know," I said at last. "It seems really creepy."

"It does, doesn't it? What's with all the signs?"

"You know, it's possible that they're just really private people. Some people are. I hate it when my mother barges into my room or looks through my drawers."

"Your mother does that?" He gave me an odd look.

"Sometimes. Doesn't yours?"

He shook his head no and we walked for a while, thinking, enjoying the easy way our steps fit together.

"Maybe she lost the baby," I suggested. That made sense to me, that they were in mourning and wanted to be alone.

"She didn't though," David said. "I talked to Mrs. Bertman this afternoon. Nothing escapes her." This was true. Mrs. Bertman is the neighbourhood news-watch. "She's the one who told me they were back. She saw them come home from the hospital, and naturally she asked. Mr. Parker said his wife was supposed to rest, but that the doctors said the baby should be okay. It's due in February."

I counted up on my fingers. "She's just three or four months then, right?"

"Right. We should talk to my mom about it."

"How come?" I felt a little jealous that he wanted to share what was ours with his mother, whom I hadn't even met.

It was then he told me about Marie, his mother. She

had practised years ago as a midwife. She wasn't trained for it exactly, but she'd delivered over a hundred babies. Occasionally she'd still be called out at odd hours of the night to go help some woman who wanted her baby to be born at home.

That night, as we walked, he told me the circumstances of his birth. Once he started, it seemed he couldn't stop, and we walked for over an hour leaving the Parkers far behind. David had never talked before, not with any of his friends, about himself, about Marie. It was something special he was trusting me to understand. And I did. Somehow I did.

Sixteen years ago Marie lived in Cincinnati and worked at a free clinic. David said that was a place people could go to get medical help without cost. She was a counsellor for runaway kids. One day a girl named Rachel came in for help. She was pregnant and broke and fourteen years old. Marie took her home with her. She had nowhere else to go and refused to talk about her parents, the people she'd run from. A few weeks later she had the baby, David, there in Marie's apartment. When he got to that part I remember how he stopped walking and looked up at the sky for a long time.

"Marie wanted her to go to the hospital to have me but she wouldn't. Marie almost never recommends the hospital for people, but she said Rachel was high risk. But she was stubborn, my mother was. And I'm glad about that. I don't even know why I should care, but I do. It makes me happy to think of her insisting on her own way." A few days later Rachel left. David stayed. Marie raised him as her own.

As he talked about Marie I realised that she and David shared something that Mom and I never have. They were friends. He admired her. He liked her. He talked to her about things that mattered to him. He asked her advice and he listened when she answered. That's not to say he followed what she said, but he listened and trusted that it was given out of love. He never called her Mom, always Marie.

Oddly enough, one of the things we had in common was the lifelong experience of hiding our familes. I had hidden my parents, or tried to, because I was faintly embarrassed by them. His was a treasure he'd guarded for a long time. He'd never told a soul. Until me. With me he shared it. Somehow, he picked me out of all the world.

"I feel really good talking to you, Liv," he said when we'd finally turned around and were headed back to my house. "You listen like it matters."

"It does," I told him, surprised at how thick with tears my throat had become.

"It's new for me. Talking like this."

"It is for me too."

"I'd like you to meet Marie. I think you two will like each other."

The truth is I didn't want to meet Marie. I was scared she would see through me, see me as shallow, as immature, as nowhere good enough for her son. And that then he would see me that way too. I didn't tell him, of course. Not then. I said, "Sure, yes, okay," and we made a plan to meet the next day, Saturday. Marie would be home in the afternoon. He looked at me a long time that night before he said goodbye. I thought he was going to kiss me, that I would kiss him, that it would be the first real kiss of my life. But instead, he stood there, under the light of the harvest moon, and looked. I looked too. At his wide brown eyes, at the crinkles in his forehead, at the planes of his cheeks.

"Thank you," he said after a long time of looking. "It's your birthday, but I feel like I'm the one who got the gift." And then he touched me, very gently, with two fingers held to my cheek. "Goodnight Liv," he said, and his voice cracked. He turned then and took off at a run. I watched his loping stride, his long legs. "See ya tomorrow," he yelled when he got to the top of Bayberry and turned the corner to his house.

"Yeah. See you tomorrow," I whispered — to him, to the moon, to the Livvie Sinclair who was newborn that night.

Sometime later, after not sleeping, after lying awake for a long, long time, restless and tingly with the thought of David, I remembered the Parkers with a pang of guilt. I saw again Mrs. Parker's pale face against her pillow and knew suddenly, absolutely, that no one like David had ever loved her.

7

Of all the things that Marie was, scary was not one of them. I was scared when I met her, as I said. Scared of what she'd think of me, of how I'd act with her. I'd never met a midwife, or even knew there were such things. I was intensely curious and equally afraid that I might stare or somehow make David regret he'd brought me home.

But Marie wasn't like that. She was so average it was a cinch getting to know her. For one thing, their house was a lot like ours. Messier, definitely, but basically normal. They had a big green couch in the living room made out of some velvety material, and two big chairs and a TV. They had a wooden dining room table like ours, but it was completely cluttered up with books and jackets and junk. My mother's was shining and empty. Marie was in the kitchen when we got there, making apple sauce. It was steamy and warm and smelled of cinnamon and apples and sugar.

"Hi," she said, waving her wooden spoon at us. She was standing at the stove wearing loose brown corduroy pants and a white fisherman's sweater. She was older than I'd imagined, older than my mother by ten years. Her hair was tied up in a scarf. What I could see was predominantly grey, with little glints still of auburn in it. When she got close, shook my hand, I saw that her eyes were brown and smiling like David's. It's remarkable that they weren't related by blood. They looked a lot alike.

She fixed us all bowls of hot apple sauce, and we sat down at the table in the kitchen. It was a little butcher-block with stools instead of chairs. "So how are you liking it here?" she asked me. "David tells me your family just moved this summer."

"It's fine," I answered, feeling awkward and relieved at the same time. It was the kind of question anybody's mother might ask. "The apple sauce's good," I told her politely.

"Well, thank you, dear. It is rather good, isn't it?" She sort of chuckled and we all ate some more.

David looked from one to the other of us like he'd just invented us both and was pleased.

"Did David tell me your mother sells Avon?"

"Yes, she does," I admitted.

"Well, good. I'll get to meet her, I hope. Your last name is what?"

"Sinclair."

"Sinclair. Okay. I really like to keep up with the neighbours, but it's hard. It seems I stay too busy between school and work."

"I didn't know you were in school," I said.

"Oh yes, and at this rate I'll be in school for the rest of my life!" She laughed, and I did too. It was contagious.

"Marie's going to be a minister," David said. "She's studying at the seminary downtown."

That time I know I stared. "Can you, uh, can you *do* that?" I asked idiotically.

She laughed again. "Can I be a minister, you mean?"

I was embarrassed, but nodded yes.

"Well, we'll see if I can. The proof is in the pudding. But yes, our church allows women ministers, if that's what you're asking. It's something I've been coming to for years, inside. Now, I'm taking the steps to make it official." She smiled gently at me.

"Oh." That was literally the most I could come up with. "My family is nothing," I finally volunteered. That sounded stupid, but it was true. We never went to church or even talked about God. It was simply not mentioned.

"Well, do you want some more apple sauce anybody?" she asked, deftly, kindly (I think) changing the subject, and getting up to go back to the stove. We both wanted more.

"Livia, *you* tell me something about this sex-ed class you two are taking. Everything David tells me sounds crazy. Nice, but crazy. Is your term project really to care about somebody? I mean, is he telling the truth?"

"Marie, you're breaking my heart," David said in a joking voice. To me he said, "She doesn't believe me. I get no respect." But he was smiling.

"It really is different," I told her. "Mrs. Fulton is doing it as an experiment. I'm not sure what she's trying to find out or how she intends to measure her results, but that's what she says — it's an experiment."

"An experiment?" Marie asked.

"That's what she said. Isn't that right?" I looked at David who nodded confirmation.

"I think her main thing is not wanting any of us to have sex or at least get pregnant while we're in high school," David said. "I imagine she'll track us down for the next three years, everyone in that class, and ask us to fill out confidential surveys about our sex lives." He and I both laughed, but almost immediately I was blushing.

"More power to her — if it works," Marie said from the stove. There was steam in her face and she looked kind of glisteny and pretty. "There's too much grief caused by children having children."

"I wouldn't be here if my mom hadn't had sex," David said.

Marie turned all the way around from the stove and stared at him. "Livia knows?" she asked. He smiled at her and nodded.

She looked at me again then, with her head slightly cocked to one side like David did and a slow smile coming into her eyes. "Well, well." She gave me a little nod and turned back to her apples. Her back to us, she continued, "You've got me in a corner on that one and you know it, kiddo. Of course I'm glad Rachel had you. I'm delighted, but, but, but . . . ." She broke off.

David winked at me. "I'm teasing you, Marie," he said.

"I know you are, and that's half of why it's so hard to say anything right. You're *laughing* at me, you goof. You know perfectly well what I mean and you're letting me dig a hole for myself out of pure and rotten meanness." She was laughing now.

David told her then about the Parkers, how he and I had chosen them together the day they moved in. I talked too, chiming in as though I'd known her all my life. Whatever initial awkwardness there'd been was gone. Marie listened closely, nodding her head up and down, asking questions. She knew the Emsley Place and had already heard neighbourhood talk about the Parkers. "So you two have chosen them for your term project? You're going to care about them?"

"That's right, only now we don't know what to do since he put up all those signs," I said.

"I've thought of a million things I could do to help them get that place ready for winter," David said. "In shop last year we had a whole section on winterising houses and installing insulation and plastic — the whole bit."

"I remember," Marie said. "You were a big help around here. But it sounds like they want to be left alone."

"I know," I admitted.

"How do you know *she* wants to be left alone?" David persisted. "That's what bugs me about this. I think *he's* the one putting up the signs. What about her?

She's the one who's pregnant, and sick too."

"But David, they're married," Marie said with great emphasis, as though that was an answer.

"So what?" he said.

"So maybe they need some time alone. I don't know what's wrong with her — it could be almost anything from what I've heard, and I've learned enough not to diagnose at a distance — but it very well may be that the best thing for her right now is rest and quiet, undisturbed time. Is that so strange?"

David shook his head and bit his bottom lip, a habit of his when he was worried. "No, that's not strange, exactly, I just have a funny feeling about it."

"Do you?" Marie asked me.

I thought about it. "I'm not sure," I said at last. "I can understand wanting to be alone; I like that too. Those signs are a little weird, but if she's sick it might even be necessary. See, I don't know if there's something strange about it or if we just think so because we had plans to help them out."

I looked over at David. It made me uncomfortable to be disagreeing with him, but I felt free, too, to speak my mind. Some part of me knew, even then, that he would rather I be honest than fakey. So I was.

"Well, that's part of it for me too, I admit," David said. "How are we going to care about them if we can't even get to meet them?"

Marie laughed. "I don't see what one has to do with the other," she said. "Your assignment is to care, right?"

We both nodded yes.

"So care." She glanced at our blank faces and went on. "I mean care, care a lot, think about them, care about them, but care enough for now to respect their wishes and do it from a distance."

So that's what we did. Or tried to do. We cared about them. It was harder than I thought it would be. How do you care about someone you don't even know? I used to think I cared about lots of people I didn't know, starving children in Africa, for instance. Now I'm not so sure I ever did. We agreed to set aside some time every day to think about them in what we hoped was a caring way. I'd sit and visualise Mrs. Parker's pale, thin face, think about her being pregnant and sick and try to care, just care. I could feel sorry for her, but I wasn't sure that was the same thing. David was concentrating on Mr. Parker, but he wasn't getting too far with it. He said for him caring was a lot like praying, but since I'd never prayed I really didn't know what he meant. Or if what I was doing was doing any good.

We saw Mr. Parker one day when he was coming home from work. We'd been sitting on the front stoop at my house when we saw him drive by. Unlike the other houses on Bayberry, the Emsley Place didn't have a driveway, just those steep ugly steps leading straight up the hill. David and I jumped up and, as casually as we could, sauntered over just as Mr. Parker was getting out of his car.

"Hi," I said, smiling and waving at him. He looked a little different from the day they moved in. For one thing, he was wearing a suit and tie. He never even slowed down, though, just started up the steps.

"Hey," David called, "we were just wondering how you and Mrs. Parker are doing. Is she feeling any better?"

Mr. Parker never even paused, never looked at either one of us. We stood there and watched his back till he was in the house, slamming the front door behind him.

"How rude," I muttered, David didn't say anything, just shook his head and put his hand on the back of my neck. His forehead was creased in the centre, he was biting his lip, and he had a pained, bewildered look in his eyes.

"Let's get out of here, David," I said, putting my arm around his waist and tugging gently. "Want to go to the creek?" I was trying to distract him. It hurt to see him like this.

Once, without breaking step, he turned around and walked backward, looking at the Emsley Place. "I wonder," he said, then shook his head.

"Yeah," I agreed, glancing at the house. "I do too." But I was lying. I wasn't thinking of the Parkers at all just then.

At the creek, David sat and threw pebbles into the brown, shallow water. We didn't talk, and eventually I stretched out on the grass and tried to care. About the Parkers. Like I was supposed to. I guess I dozed instead. Slowly, I became aware that David was tickling me on the cheek with a twig.

"Hello," I said, opening my eyes.

"Are you caring?" he asked.

"Sort of. It's really hard to do this in the abstract."

"I know. I've been trying to put myself in that guy's place. And I can't do it. I don't understand what's going on with him."

"Yeah, really. This whole thing would be easier if we could at least meet them."

David lay beside me, looking at the sky for a long time, without speaking. "I keep thinking," he said at last, "that if you were . . . Well, I mean, if *I* had a wife who was sick. Oh, hell, I don't know. I just don't get it."

He smiled at me then and I could see his mood had changed, lifted somehow. Mine did too, because I understood what he'd been thinking. If I were his wife.

Mrs. Fulton asked the class one day how the caring projects were going. We'd only been at it a few weeks. Helen was caring about her grandmother who was in a nursing home. She said she'd been enjoying listening to stories about how rotten her father was as a kid. That seemed so easy and so rewarding. I told Mrs. Fulton that caring was a whole lot harder than I'd suspected it would be. She didn't ask any questions, just smiled at me real warmly and said that if I'd discovered that *already*, I was certainly on the right track.

I didn't think so. For one thing, it was boring just thinking about them. For another, I was caring so much about David that the gap between my feelings for him and my feeling for the Parkers was so big as to be an embarrassment.

8

And then the blasting started. A decision had been made by the city council to widen the highway that pased by High Ridge. To do that, they had to blast away part of the hillside that backed up to the Parkers' property. That first blast sounded like a bomb going off, but much louder than on TV. I was still asleep when it hit and it jerked me awake so quickly I practically fell out of bed. I heard Mom downstairs give a little shocked scream and Dad say, "What the — " Not five minutes later there was another one that set the windows rattling. I got dressed and went down.

"What's going on?" I asked Mom, who was sitting at the kitchen table drinking coffee.

"It's the blasting for the highway," she told me in a thin, pained voice. "I knew they were going to widen it, but I never thought it would be like this." She was rubbing her forehead like she had a headache. Dad came in then and told us that he'd found out from some of the neighbours that it was expected to continue for at least a month. Another blast hit just then and we all held our breath. We could hear dishes clinking in the cupboard.

I've been in cars all my life, driving down highways that were cut through mountains or that ran through hills, and never thought once about what it took to make them. This was just an expansion, not even the original cut, but what a racket. The worst part for me was that we never knew when it would hit. Somedays there would be twenty blasts before noon and then nothing for the whole afternoon and then at, say, four o'clock there would be three or four more. There was no way to prepare for it and no way, for me at least, just to tune it out.

David's the one who first noticed what was happening to the Parkers' house — the cement foundation that held it up had begun to divide. There was one big crack that ran right through the middle of it and lots of spidery offshoots. Their house was much older and much closer to the actual blasting site than any other in the subdivision, and it appeared they were suffering the heaviest damage. We were pretty sure that Mr. Parker had noticed it too because we saw him out in front of the house one day, looking. We hadn't tried to talk to him again, but we both kept pretty close watch. Mostly we were watching for Mrs. Parker, but she never even came out on the porch, at least not when we were there to see.

It was by accident that I actually met her. I can't say it was luck (although it felt like that at the time), because nothing about knowing Maggie Parker was lucky. And I don't want to think it was Divine Providence, because if it was, it's just one more thing to hate God for. If there is a God. I call it an accident.

Mom and I had gone out together to do errands at this shopping centre near us that has a supermarket and a drugstore right next to it. She was getting food and I'd volunteered to pick up some medicine her doctor had called in. She was getting bad headaches. I was in the check-out line when I noticed that the woman in front of me had a bee crawling around in her hair. It was late September and the bees had gone sluggish and stupid. Her hair was swept up in a bun and the bee appeared to be trapped in the folds. I was right behind her and I could hear this angry buzzing sound, so I know she could. But she was making no effort to get it out. I tapped her on the shoulder and said, "Ma'am?" When she turned around I realised it was Mrs. Parker.

"Yes?" she said in a very tired, kind of throaty voice.

"You have a bee in your hair."

She just looked at me for a moment. Her eyes were deep, deep blue and hung with dark circles. "I know I do," is what she finally said.

"Would you like me to help you get it out?"

Her eyes widened perceptibly. "Could you?"

"Well, hold still." Carefully, I reached up into her hair and found the clip that was holding it. "Easy now," I said, talking, I think, to both of us. Very slowly, I managed to unclip it without disturbing the bee. As her hair fell down — it was about shoulder length — the bee flew out. It buzzed heavily, flying in confused, slow circles heading toward the windows. A man behind us swatted at it with a newspaper.

She sighed and I could hear a trembling in her breath. "Thank you, oh thank you," she said in a low voice. "It's been in there ever since I left the house, but I was afraid to get it out myself for fear of getting stung. Isn't that silly?" She made a little laugh, but I could tell she'd really been afraid.

She didn't look one bit pregnant. She was very thin and there was a greyish cast to her skin, past pale. Her hair was dark brown and kind of curly but it looked dull. She was wearing a shirtwaist dress and there were no bulges.

"You're Mrs. Parker, aren't you?" I said on impulse. She was almost up to the checker and I didn't want to lose this chance.

"Yes. I am." She turned and looked me in the eye. "How did you know?"

"I'm Livvie Sinclair. I live right up the street from you on Bayberry. We've been wondering how you are. You know, I mean, how you're doing." With embarrassment and then dismay, I realised she was buying a box of sanitary napkins. I assumed she must have lost the baby, a possibility that hadn't occurred to me since I'd really started thinking about her, caring. I always thought of her pregnant. I'd taken Mrs. Bertman's news as gospel.

"I'm glad to meet you, Livvie," she said. "I'm doing much better. Thank you for asking." She spoke as if these were lines in a play, slowly, a script she was just learning.

She took her turn at the checkout, and I was afraid she would leave, walk off, go back into that house and I'd never see her again. But she didn't. She finished at the cash register and stood to one side waiting for me, looking shy and sort of scared. I couldn't tell how old she was: twenty-five? thirty? I'm not too good at judging people's ages, but there was something worn about her, something very, very tired.

I walked over to where she stood waiting. She smiled at me and I smiled back. "Well, thanks again, Livvie," she said. "I appreciate it that you helped me out. That dumb bee had been in there crawling around and buzzing for over an hour. I kept waiting for it to sting me and get it over with. I just didn't know how to ask someone to help me get it out." She shrugged her shoulders. "I guess you know, I'm new around here."

"Yeah, I remember when you moved in."

"Pretty dramatic entrance wasn't it?" We both laughed.

"I'm pretty new too," I told her. "We just moved here about a month before you did."

"Did you really?" She sounded amazed.

"Yeah. Right in time for the blasting." I said it lightly, as though it was a joke, but I'd often wondered about how the blasts had felt for her. Their house was the closest of all and was splitting at its very base.

Mrs. Parker stared down at the floor. She did it so suddenly that I found myself looking too. She was wearing knee-high leather boots. I was wearing tennis shoes. Very softly she said, "That blasting's about to drive me right straight out of my head, I swear it." There was some undertone that made me believe she meant it.

"Mrs. Parker?" I found my own voice matched hers now for softness. We were two odd conspirators in the Rexall. "I'd be happy to come visit you sometime if you wouldn't mind."

She kept staring at the floor, even when she answered me. "Well, thank you. I'd like that very much. Please call me Maggie. I didn't realise people were so neighbourly around here."

I felt like telling her that nobody had much of a chance with those signs up, but I didn't. She put out her hand for me to shake and I was surprised by how tiny and cold it felt — like little bird bones.

Suddenly, I felt shy too. Inviting myself over had been forward, but it was more than that. Here she'd been my project for almost a month and we'd never spoken. She had no idea how much I had been thinking about her, how many hours David and I had spent talking about her, speculating. There was something else too. Being with her, even for just those few minutes, I found I really did care about her. There was a weight on her that was almost visible and I felt tugged.

We talked for a few more minutes, standing there by the drugstore doors, neither one of us in a hurry to leave. She did know about the crack in the foundation, in fact she told me she'd called the highway department to report it. She said Mr. Emsley had been a great-uncle of hers. The house had been handed down to her mother who'd never lived in it, and then passed on to her when her mother died, which had been recently.

"My husband got a job up here and it seemed like a blessing, having the house and all. We were ready to . . . to make a change." She looked like she wanted to say something more, like she was hungry to talk but didn't quite know how.

"I'm sorry you lost the baby," I blurted out without meaning to.

"But I didn't," she said. "Is that what you thought when I fainted that day in the street?"

I nodded. It seemed impossible to explain that I'd heard through Mrs. Bertman she was still pregnant when she got home from the hospital, but that I'd assumed, seeing the sanitary napkins, that she was having her period.

"You see, I had some haemorrhaging and I'm still bleeding a little, but I'm pregnant." She patted her abdomen with one hand and smiled.

"Well, Mrs. Parker, Maggie, if there's anything at all I can do to help, I'd be happy to. Really. So would David."

She smiled. "Who's David?"

"He's um, sort of, you know . . . "

"Your boyfriend?"

"Well, you might say that."

"Livvie, you've already done something for me and

I thank you. I'd be happy if you *and* David" — she smiled again — "would like to come visit me sometime. I could really use the company."

Just then, through the window, I spotted my mother wheeling groceries out to our car. Had I cared well about Maggie, I would have introduced them. For weeks I'd suspected she might be lonely, and talking to her had confirmed it. Mom could have been company for her too, better company than I probably, but I didn't want her in on this. The Parkers belonged to David and me. We might talk to Marie about them every now and then, but we kept them to ourselves. I said goodbye and asked when would be a good time to come. She told me after school on Monday. So it was set.

9

I didn't realise how small Maggie Parker was until I saw her beside David. She only came up to his shoulders, maybe not even that. When she answered the door that Monday afternoon, she looked tiny and tired. At first, we all stood awkwardly in the entrance hall not knowing how to begin. Then she invited us into the living room, and David and I sat stiffly on the couch.

"I guess you've seen the house, haven't you?" she asked, gesturing vaguely at the room. For a moment I thought she knew that we'd spied on her that one night, but then she continued. "Dean says half the neighbourhood was up here the day we moved in."

"We were trying to help," David said. "We saw you take sick."

"It was a great kindness," she answered. There was something unsaid; I could sense it, but I didn't know what it was. "Dean says I'll do anything to get out of work." She gave a short laugh. "Of course he's just kidding," she added hurriedly.

"Are you feeling any better?" David asked.

"Yes, some. But I can't keep anything down," Maggie said. "I keep throwing up."

"Morning sickness," I pronounced. "It's only supposed to last a few weeks." We'd just finished studying the stages of pregnancy in Mrs. Fulton's class and I really thought I knew all about it.

Maggie shook her head at me. "It's not just mornings. It's morning, afternoon, and night. And it's not just nausea, it's vomiting. I can't hold anything down. Anything."

David was looking at her closely, nodding his head very slightly. "What does your doctor say?" he asked.

"He gave me some medicine, but I can't take it. Nothing stays down," Maggie told him.

"It sounds pretty severe," he said gently. "Have you been losing weight?" His voice was quiet and certain. Did he learn this from his mother, from Marie? I was amazed by his calm, his sensitivity.

Maggie nodded her head and started to cry. I felt frightened and uncomfortable. I was unused to seeing people cry back then. She was sitting across from us in a big blue chair which seemed to engulf her. She looked so small and so sick, sitting there crying, wiping her eyes with her sleeve. "I'm sorry," she said at last, hiccupping like a child. "I'm really scared. I've lost seventeen pounds in the last three months. I don't know how the baby's going to make it if this keeps up."

"That's a lot," David said in that tender tone. I felt cold all through. At least he knew something to say, and his manner, his voice, his face, all of it seemed right. He wasn't afraid of what was going on, he wasn't shocked by it or put off. He wanted to help; I wanted to disappear.

"I'm bleeding too," Maggie said in a small voice.

"I know, Livvie told me," David said, squeezing my hand. Maggie looked up then at me and smiled, the blue of the chair deepening the wet blue of her eyes. I smiled back, stiff with discomfort.

"It's not at all what it's supposed to be. I have these wonderful books about pregnancy. Lots of them. And none of them say anything about a situation like this." She shrugged. "If this baby makes it, I'll have to write my own. It'll make medical history." She grinned.

Just then a blast tore through the room. The very air around us seemed to lurch and vibrate with the noise. Maggie winced, eyes shut tight. The window panes rattled, and the chandelier in the hallway tinkled ominously. Up there, in that house, it was worse.

"Good Lord," David whistled when it was over. "It's nothing like this over at our house, and I just live a couple of blocks away."

"I know," Maggie said. "This house is in exactly the wrong place. The shock waves or whatever they call them, hit us very hard. I'm not sure the house is going to stand up to it."

"Yeah, we saw the crack in the foundation," David told her. "It seems to me you ought to be able to sue for that or something. Something."

"Well, I've called about it. The Highway Department gave me the name of the engineering company that's doing the actual work and they gave me the name of the insurance company and they gave me the name of somebody else. It's a big run-around as far as I can tell, but they did say they would send somebody out to assess the damage." She sighed and looked out the window, out toward the highway. "That would be a big job, wouldn't it?" she said in a kind of dreamy voice, "assessing the damage."

No one will ever be able properly to assess the damage done. It is beyond what can be measured. But that day, when we left, David and I were certain we could help.

We came again the next day and the day after that. Marie listened to our report of Maggie's symptoms and made an herb tea she said might help with the nausea. We delivered it. We gathered a basket of windfall apples and took them to her. She was delighted with them. She and I made apple pies one afternoon while David unloaded cartons of books and put them on shelves for her. She didn't explain why her husband hadn't done this weeks before and we didn't ask. We never asked about Mr. Parker and she almost never mentioned him. At five-thirty or six o'clock she would look nervously at her watch and say she thought it was time we left and would we come again tomorrow, any day at all. Any weekday. It was understood that *he* was home on the weekends and that we shouldn't come then.

10

We went to see Maggie almost every day after school. The more time we spent with her the easier it was to care. We liked her. She had been raised in Georgia and had a slow, funny, drawling way of speaking. She wouldn't talk much about her family, said simply, "It was a mess." We were curious; we wanted to know more, but Maggie wasn't a person we were willing to push. She had a way of dropping a subject that wasn't to be trifled with, and we didn't. She did mention once that she was one of eleven children, which was hard for either David or me to imagine.

One day we were up there helping her with the cleaning. David moved furniture around and I vacuumed behind it. Ordinarily I hate housework, but doing it with David, for Maggie, made it fun, like an adventure. It was early in October and hot; summer didn't want to give up that year. We were taking a rest, sitting in front of the fan and drinking lemonade, when the front doorbell rang. It had an empty, haunting sound; the chimes were discordant and creaky with disuse. We were all startled. Maggie took a deep breath and stood up.

"Well, who on earth?" she said. "We haven't had many visitors." As if this could be news to us. David and I stood up too and walked with her to the door.

It was a man from an insurance company, sent by the State Highway Department. He was short and squat, wearing a grey coat and a grey felt hat. He looked like a cop or a gangster from an old movie. He introduced himself and briefly tipped his hat at Maggie. She didn't introduce us, but reached over and held onto my hand. I knew she wanted us to stay.

"I didn't expect you, but I'm very glad you're here," she said to him carefully.

He carried a clipboard and a pencil. "I'm sorry I didn't call," he said, clearing his throat, "but with my schedule I wasn't sure when I'd be able to fit you in. And today, I had a slot open — so here I am."

Maggie led the four of us from room to room never once letting go of my hand. She showed him a large crack running from floor to ceiling in their dining room. Plaster hung in patches along the length of it. Upstairs, in the baby's room, which looked out over the subdivision, there were two cracked panes of glass. There was a crib and a dresser; the rest was packed in boxes. There were no curtains up then, just the high, empty windows. I had the feeling she was showing these things to David and me as well. Standing there, I could see my house.

She led us outside. In back of the house ran a narrow

sidewalk, directly below where David and I had crouched in the apple orchard. There was a large ugly crack in the back wall and in the sidewalk as well. The man took notes and Maggie glanced over at him from time to time to make sure he was getting it all down.

The very worst damage was to the foundation in the front. A long jagged line cut through it. Were it to crack further, the front porch and perhaps the whole house would cave in. I had a brief vision of the Emsley Place careening down the hill to the foot of Bayberry Court. "That's new," Maggie said, pointing at the crack. "It wasn't here when we moved in." David nodded in confirmation and the insurance man looked at it carefully and wrote something on his pad.

"What about the basement?" he asked, nodding toward a small green door in the foundation wall. He looked hot and uncomfortable in his suit and hat. The afternoon sun was glaring.

"I don't know," Maggie said, "I've never been in there." Still holding my hand, pulling me along, she walked to the door, which hung at an awkward angle. There was a place for a padlock but the door was unlocked and completely unguarded except by cobwebs. Maggie stood staring, as if uncertain how to proceed, so with a quick thump of my hip, I opened it for her.

Inside, it was thirty degrees cooler, damp and very dark. At first, all four of us stood dumbly, adjusting to the darkness. At the very back, where the house abuts the hill, the wall was dirt, not concrete. Low wood beams hung with hoses and rakes and sinewy electrical cords ran the length of the house. Rickety metal shelves held old canning jars and pots, cardboard boxes, discarded lamps and clocks, radios. And dust. Dust blanketed everything, but the smell was dank, as though it were almost but not quite ready to go to mud.

As I turned, the light from the door blinded me and, blinking, I saw David momentarily silhouetted against a wall. I couldn't make out the features on his face, but I sensed he was looking at me. "Hi," I said weakly.

"Livvie?" He came toward me gingerly, picking through a maze of boards, parts of motors, broken kitchen chairs. I wanted to let go of Maggie's hand, to hold David's. He seemed the safest thing in there. But Maggie held tight, her bony little hand sticky and cold. I could not let her go.

David came close and rubbed my back, just once as though to say, I'm here. It's all right. To Maggie, he whispered, "I think you've got a great case." She found his eyes in the darkness and smiled.

The insurance man studied the cement wall for a long time and finally said, "Okay." We filed out into the bright, hot, dry yard and again stood silent a moment, the four of us. Maggie had her free hand up shielding her eyes, looking at the insurance man. He squinted at his notepad and wrote something more. And then a buzz went on in the back of my eyes.

That doesn't sound right, does it? Buzzes should go on, or off, in people's ears. But it was my eyes. Or maybe both at the same time. Like a blinking light with an alarm buzzer, but I saw the blink before I heard it. And what blinked was not light, but an absence of light. Black. A black line. A thick, black line. Close. And all the time the buzz of it, the alarm was getting stronger, louder. Snake. Snake. My eyes jolted into fast focus and I saw it clearly, not three feet away — a gleaming black snake as thick as a fence post and twice as long.

Perhaps Maggie saw it at the same moment, or perhaps the shock in my body translated into hers with lightning speed. She gasped, screamed, and dug her fingers into the palm of my hand. In a blur we ran, both of us, never letting go, off the grass and up the steep, tilting stairs onto the front porch and through the door, into the front hall where we stood breathing heavily. A short second later the door flew open again and the insurance man ran in. He avoided our eyes and within moments we were all laughing shakily.

"I hate snakes," the man said. "Been that way all my life."

"Oh, I know, me too," Maggie offered, still gasping for breath. "Course, it was only a black snake wasn't it, and they're harmless. But still ... oouh." She was white. Her lips looked like a chalk and the only colour at all on her face was the bluish black shadows of her eyes.

"Where's David?" I asked, suddenly aware of his absence.

The insurance man laughed. "I just ran," he said apologetically. We all had.

I went back out on the porch and leaned over the rail. Below me, on the lawn, David stood looking thoughtfully at the basement door. The snake was gone.

"Are you okay?" I asked, feeling idiotic. Of course he was. He was standing there.

He looked up and smiled at me. "Yeah, I'm fine. Are you?"

"I got so scared. I feel pretty stupid," I told him.

He came around to the steps and climbed them easily two at a time. But not even he, with his long legs, could take that top step two at a time — it was perversely higher than the others and sloped in a way that threw you back on yourself, back toward the concrete. I took his hand.

"Hey," he said gently, "snakes are like that. They give you a start."

"That was more than a start, David. Maggie and I both panicked."

"So did Whatsisname," he said with a low chuckle. "I thought he was going to knock you two down getting up the steps."

We went into the house. Whatsisname was getting ready to leave. He had closed his notebook and was tucking it into an inside pocket in his jacket. "Is it gone?" he asked David as we entered. David nodded yes. "I just hate snakes," he said again, this time to David.

We watched him out the door and down the steps, first to the level of the lawn and then down again the two stairways that wound to the street. There was something comical about the way he kept turning his head, how obviously nervous he was. I'd been scared too, but then, from the safety of that high porch, it seemed silly.

"He says the blasting on the highway is probably driving the snakes out of the hillside," Maggie said, her gaze also following his descent. There was some longing in her eyes as though she wanted to be with him, leaving.

"Well, that makes sense," David said. "That and the dry weather. In a drought they come out looking for water. With this blasting going on I'd say all the living things on this hillside are pretty turned around."

"Yes. I feel that way," Maggie answered quietly.

David and I both looked at her then, drawn I think by the absolute despair in her voice. She looked alarmingly ill — white, drained, frail. "Where did it go?" she asked David.

He sighed and I knew he didn't want to say it. "Under the house. Into the basement."

She shuddered and stared at her feet, at the green planking of the porch. "We're standing right over it. Maybe over a whole den of them," she said, her voice rising like a scared child's. I could feel my toes curl upward in revulsion at the thought of standing over a den of snakes.

"Well, I doubt that," David said. He put a hand on her shoulder and guided her off the porch and back into the house.

We walked through the hallway to the kitchen. Maggie sat down and I went to the sink and poured her a glass of water. She looked frighteningly trembly and sick.

David talked to her, to both of us, about black snakes. They were considered a lucky snake by some people. How anyone could consider himself lucky to have a snake at all is beyond me, but that's what he said. They eat rodents. Chances are, he was saying, the snake was disoriented from the blasting and had come to their basement because it was cool and dark and moist. It would leave soon; there was no nest down there.

Suddenly Maggie bolted. She shot from her chair and was gone. David and I stared at each other in bewilderment and then, in the silence, we heard her retching in the bathroom.

When we left there that afternoon, Maggie was huddled shivering under a thick down comforter. It was eighty degrees outside, but she was freezing. She'd emerged from the bathroom with her teeth chattering and I'd helped her into bed, going back for a cool wet cloth for her forehead.

11

Maggie Parker became real for us that day, and in the days and weeks and months that followed we would never again be able to think of her as a project. She was a person, a sick and frightened woman on the verge of losing her baby. Later, we knew she was on the verge of losing more than that, but by then our lives were so entangled we were beyond what help knowing something can be. We lost our perspective about Maggie. Is it right to have perspective about people? Hirsch says it is, says it's necessary for mental health, for self protection, for survival. I hate survival. At any rate, we had none.

Maggie wanted us there; that much is clear. She treated us as friends, very valuable friends. And David and I considered ourselves such. We both felt protective of her. Is it strange that she was at least ten years older than us and we took care of her like she was our little sister? Thinking about it now I can see it was.

Although Maggie joked about it, it became clear she was deeply frightened of snakes. She'd looked black snakes up in an encyclopaedia and found that they often nest with poisonous vipers like copperheads and rattlers. David assured her there were no rattlers around, and she would nod and say "No, of course not" but then gaze off unconvinced. Once she told me she'd dreamed she was taking long low pans of water up on the hillside as an offering to them: Stay away from my house, drink here, leave us alone.

David and I did see another snake that fall, slithering its way up the hill and under the house. David grew very serious and said he thought it was a copperhead. We said nothing about it to Maggie, although I felt strange keeping silent. We didn't think she could handle it, and we were taking care of her.

One day David and I talked to Mrs. Fulton after school. It was mid-term, and our turn to meet with her about our caring project. She met with everyone in the class to see how things were going. After her conference, Helen told me it was the first time in her whole life she'd had a private conversation with a teacher.

Mrs. Fulton sat listening to us quietly, nodding her head up and down and looking from David to me and back again. Her eyes widened when we told about the snake and Maggie's reaction to it.

"It's as though she can't relax, can't forget it," I said. "She's really frightened. More than normal. I mean snakes are scary. I was scared too, but she can't let it go."

"She's obsessive," David began, but I jumped back in, interrupting him.

"Yes. Exactly. Even when she's not talking about it, you can see she's jumpy. She's watching for them everywhere."

"Where's her husband?" Mrs. Fulton asked. "Can't he do something?"

So we told her then, reluctantly, about the signs, the signs we passed every day now. The signs Mr. Parker put up.

"You mean he doesn't want you up there?" Mrs. Fulton began to squint, narrowing her eyes at us.

"We don't really know what he wants," I explained. "We never see him and she never talks about him, so neither do we."

Mrs. Fulton took a deep breath and let it out slowly. Her mouth was tightly pursed and she seemed about to speak but decided not to. Instead she looked out the window for a long time, frowning. "Caring is a risky business," she said at last. "Be careful."

We were warned. Let that be said, Hirsch. We were warned.

Mrs. Fulton asked us then how we liked working together. David and I both squirmed a little and smiled. I, predictably, blushed. "It's good," David said at last. "At least I think so, don't you Livvie?"

"I do. I mean, I think it's fine," I said, feeling like an idiot.

"It looks like you're both enjoying it," Mrs. Fulton said smiling at us and rocking back in her chair a little.

David caught my eye just then and smiled again. "Yeah, it's going fine."

"What are you learning?" Mrs. Fulton asked.

Now this felt like a trick question. What did she expect us to be learning? To care about somebody? Later in the year, when she was just teaching biology, we knew exactly what we were supposed to be learning — phyla, cell structure, whatever — it was clear. We could study for it. And with lots of stuff in sex-ed, like anatomy and birth control statistics, there were lists we could memorise, so we knew what she expected. But with the caring project it was really undefined. She said she wasn't sure what we were supposed to learn, but she was interested in whatever we *did* discover. There really wasn't a right answer. And that was hard for me to get used to.

Actually, there were lots of times in that class when no one knew what the right answer was. Mrs. Fulton had a book full of these so-called value clarification exercises. She would throw out opinions or statements and let us react. We were supposed to get clear about how we felt or why we thought a certain way. I don't think it worked too well for me, because I usually ended up more muddled after we'd discussed something than before. I envy people who are perfectly sure of themselves. It must be wonderful to know you're right.

The day she first introduced this value clarification stuff Mrs. Fulton handed out a picture. It was a black and white line drawing of what was obviously an old hag. The woman was crouched over and wearing a scarf on the head. She had a long, thick nose and a pointy chin buried deep into an old coat. When she finished passing these out, Mrs. Fulton said, "Okay, raise your hand if you see the young lady." David and Helen and a good third of the class raised their hands. I was amazed and immediately checked out their papers to see if we were looking at the same thing. We were. Mrs. Fulton then asked, "Do the rest of you see the old woman?" which was some relief. "Okay. Everybody find someone who sees the woman you don't see," she instructed, "and work with them until you can all see them both."

David and Helen traced the lines of the young woman. "She's facing that way, idiot," Helen kept saying, meaning away from me. "Look. That's her ear, that's her eyelash. Tell me the truth, do you see it?" And suddenly I did. Suddenly, I could see them both, flashing back and forth. What had been the old lady's nose was the young lady's chin. The old lady's mouth — a grim slit of a line — was the young lady's choker. I laughed out loud when it hit me and proceeded to show them the old lady. All over the room, the same thing was happening. "Aha!" "Oh yeah." "Far out." I could hear it spreading. Mrs. Fulton stood at the front rocking back on her heels and smiling at us all.

When everyone was finished she asked us, "What do you think this has to do with sex education?" Good question.

"Well, it's about women," someone volunteered.

She laughed. "Anything else?"

"I guess we're all looking at the same thing and seeing something different," Helen said.

"So right you are," Mrs. Fulton beamed at her. "Now what does that have to do with sex-ed?"

"Beauty is in the eye of the beholder?" Helen smiled, knowing that wasn't it.

"Well, that's true too. Anything else?"

I knew then what she was asking for. Knew it for certain and raised my hand.

"Livvie?"

"There can be more than one right answer to a question. It depends on your point of view."

"Bravo. That's exactly what I was getting at. Many, many questions about sexuality don't have just one answer. Not a factual one anyway. People have to figure out what's right for them as individuals. Something could be right for certain people in the context of their family, their religion, or where they are in their lives. But it could be totally wrong for someone else. In here we're going to sound out a lot of different questions. Some of you will be certain that your point of view is the right one, even the only one. Keep this picture as a reminder — there may be another way to see it."

Too bad Mr. Tate wasn't in there for the Old Lady/Young Lady introduction. Mr. Tate was the principal, and he definitely did not understand the idea that there could be more than one way to look at an issue. He showed up one day about ten minutes after class had started, saying, "Don't mind me, don't mind me." Mrs. Fulton just smiled at him and waved him to a seat. Although no real trouble ever erupted about her teaching sex-ed, there were plenty of whispers and grumbles and raised eyebrows around school, and from what I could gather, among parents. Mr. Tate had come to check us out.

That day we were just getting set to do the Four Corners exercise. Mrs. Fulton would paste up these signs in the four corners of the room: Strongly Agree, Agree, Disagree, and Strongly Disagree. Then she would read statements that were designed to provoke us into taking a stance and we were supposed to go to the corner of the room that most closely represented our position. From there we could try to persuade people in other corners over to our opinion. The issues she picked were charged — pornography, premarital sex, abortion, whatever.

I loved Four Corners because, for one thing, you got to get up and move around. For another, it was fun arguing with people. The only rule was that we were supposed to be respectful, and basically we were, but there were times when it got pretty hot. Mrs. Fulton explained the game briefly to Mr. Tate and invited him to play, but he said no, he'd just watch. So she read the statement. "A woman shouldn't be allowed to have an abortion without the father's consent." As usual there was a pause and some moaning and then we were up and at it.

I went over to Disagree. David, I noticed, picked Agree. We smiled at each other. Playing these value games had given all of us practice at considering opinions we disagreed with. Mrs. Fulton started with the people in the Strongly Agree corner.

"Well, I'm here because I don't believe in abortion at all," said a girl named Becky. "As you all know, I consider it murder. Under any circumstances." We did know too. We'd gotten into a near riot the week before over the abortion issue. "What if the father is willing to support the baby, and never even knows about it because the girl goes off and aborts? It's wrong and in this case, it's not fair to either the baby or the guy."

"I agree with her about the fairness issue," said one of the boys in that corner. "If I father a child, whether it's by accident or not, I want the chance to decide, at least in part, what's going to happen."

"Absolutely. Good point," Mr. Tate said from the table where he sat. We all looked at him.

"Have you decided to play?" Mrs. Fulton asked.

"No, no. Don't mind me. I just think that's a very good point."

"Well, I think it stinks," Helen said. She was in Strongly Disagree. "The woman is the one who gets pregnant. It's the woman who gets dumped on with the whole responsibility of having sex. She's the one who has to bear the weight of it either way, whether she has an abortion or has the baby. *She's* the one who has to live with it, not the guy."

"She may not even know who the father is," said another girl in that corner. "Have you considered that?

What are you going to do — go around polling every Tom, Dick, and Harry on the street? 'Excuse me, in your opinion, should we allow Ms. X to have an abortion?' It's none of their business. Period." She looked furious.

This was pretty close to my opinion so I decided to jump in. One thing that class taught me was if I wanted to be heard I had to speak up. We weren't supposed to interrupt each other but we usually did. "Look," I said loudly, "for the most part I agree that if people have sex it's both of their responsibilities. That includes any unforeseen consequences such as pregnancy. For the most part. But what about cases of rape or incest, where the pregnancy results from sex that was unfair in the first place? What about that? The man is still the father, but he shouldn't have the right to decide what the woman does about the pregnancy."

David smiled at me and to my utter delight walked over to my corner. "You've got a convert, Livvie," Mrs. Fulton said.

"I hadn't considered rape or incest," David explained. "I have to agree with her there, although I still think, in general, the father has rights."

I was blushing like an absolute fool and missed the rest of the discussion on that point. It felt so good actually to convince David of something. Suddenly I heard Mr. Tate saying, "What about the parents? What about that?"

"What do you mean?" Mrs. Fulton asked.

"I mean if a fifteen-year-old girl got pregnant don't

you think her parents should have some say about what happens?"

"Oh. Well, that's a slightly different question. Class, let's use that one. Um, let me think how to phrase it. Okay. 'A minor should not be allowed to have an abortion without her parents' consent.' How's that? Or what about birth control? Maybe we can diffuse the abortion issue for a minute and focus on birth control. 'A minor should not be allowed to obtain birth control without his or her parents' consent.' Yes. Let's try that one." She wrote it on the board.

The entire class moved to either Disagree or Strongly Disagree. Mr. Tate stared at us. He was geting splotchy red patches on his neck. "I don't think this question provides much discussion because they all seem pretty unanimous in their disagreement," Mrs. Fulton said mildly.

"Now wait a minute," Mr. Tate said. "Some of those birth control methods can be pretty dangerous, right? How would you feel if your child ended up in the hospital because some doctor had prescribed something *so she could have sex* and you didn't even know about it?"

"I never heard of ending up in the hospital because your rubber got stuck," said one of the boys. "Help me doctor, I can't get it off,'"

"I was talking about girls," Mr. Tate said in a controlled voice that cut through our laughter.

"Oh, I get it," Helen said in her most sarcastic tone. "It's okay if boys get their condoms at the drugstore or at the gas station, but if a girl wants to get a more reliable method of birth control, she needs to have a note from Mommy. Right?"

"Mrs. Fulton, do you realise these are mere children in here talking about birth control, rape, abortion, sex? Do you really think this is appropriate?"

"I think for mere children they're doing an excellent job of considering the issues and their implications. Don't you? We've heard some good reasoning in here today. And," she smiled at us, "some good listening. Tomorrow we start our section on sexual orientation. Pick up your handouts from my desk. You might like to come back for that Mr. Tate. One point we'll certainly cover will be homosexual school teachers. Myth and fact. You're welcome any time. Class dismissed."

Mr. Tate looked like hell. He was red in the face and there was a twitch starting up in his left eye. He never did come back, and no official action was ever taken about Mrs. Fulton's class. Funny how everyone missed the really dangerous stuff. No one ever thought twice about the caring projects. They weren't even controversial. Nice, easy kid stuff, right? Care.

When she asked us at the conference what we were learning by working together, I knew it was one of those questions — like values — that depended on your point of view.

"Well," David said, "about the working together part, I'm learning it's really nice to have someone to talk things over with. I mean Livvie and I talk about it and I'm glad we do. It wouldn't be the same telling someone who wasn't there what was going on. Livvie and I are there together and it's a . . ." he seemed to be searching, "a relief. You know?"

"Yes. I think I do know," Mrs. Fulton said. "What about you, Livvie? I hope you're not learning to let David do all your talking for you."

"No, not at all," I said and giggled a little, thinking about how much I did talk with David. There were times I barely let him get a word in edgewise. "I guess I'm learning that it isn't as simple to help someone as I'd always assumed it was. With Mrs. Parker, with Maggie, I'm getting confused."

"How so?" Mrs. Fulton asked.

"Well, in a way I think we are helping but I'm not sure how. Actually, I'm not even sure what's wrong. I mean, I know there's something wrong with her health. She's having a hard pregnancy; I know that, and I'm learning all the symptoms." We'd already told her that morning sickness didn't come close to describing what Maggie Parker had. "But it seems to me there's something else wrong, something that we're helping, but I don't know how. I'm not making sense, am I?"

"Yes, you are," David said. "It's something with him, isn't it?"

"Who? Her husband?" Mrs. Fulton asked sharply.

I nodded. "Yes. There's something weird going on about him, but I can't figure it out."

"Be careful," she said again, giving us her serious green-eyed squint.

And that's where we left it at mid-term. Mrs. Fulton

urged us to feel free to talk again even if there wasn't a scheduled conference. She said she could tell we were learning a lot.

When the heat wave finally broke, Maggie began to gain weight. She was able to hold down bits of food, soup, drinks. She still didn't look pregnant to me, but some of the ghostly hollowness of her face began to fade and fill in. One day late in October, it began to rain, the first time in weeks. There was even something like a chill again in the air. We sat in her kitchen listening to the rain on the roof, watching it come down. Their yard ran brown with mud from the cut in the highway.

"It's a mess, isn't it?" Maggie asked us.

"Maybe come spring I could re-seed it for you," David said. "I think they'll be done with the blasting by then."

"Surely by then," she said. "Surely."

David and I saw Maggie almost every day and always left just before Mr. Parker came home. Sometimes we would sit on the steps of my house and watch him drive down Bayberry. He was a scowling, unapproachable man, ugly I thought, and mean. It seemed to me that he was the beast and she the beauty he kept locked away. There was something wonderful about tricking him, seeing Maggie on the sly, helping her in secret. David and I were the good elves who came when he was away, who lightened her load without his knowing, who made her life easier, or so we hoped. She needed us, and David and I had an excess of good will. Of love. So it was in the beginning.

THE MIDDLE

12

We didn't think of her all the time. Not all of it. There were times we thought only of ourselves and each other, of the we that we were forming, becoming.

The first time we kissed was in November. I'm glad we didn't kiss right away, that we waited as long as we did. From early on we'd held hands, touched, little things. It felt so good. Mrs. Fulton once asked our class did we think holding hands was a sexual act. A lot of kids sneered, but I knew better. I knew the answer to that one. It could be. It depended on who you held hands with, and how.

But the kissing. Oh yes. It was sexual for sure. We were outside. It seems most of the time we had together, alone, was outside walking. We were coming home from a dance at school. David had his arm around my shoulder, tucking me into his side. I loved it when he did that. My mother had driven us there and offered to pick us up too, but we said no. David promised her he'd get me home safely by midnight. High Ridge wasn't far from the school —

after all, we walked it every day.

The dance was fun — noisy, light, and loud with music that drove us both on and on. What fun to be in a crowd with him, jouncing up against other people and moving back, always back to each other. There was so much energy in the dancing, so much fun. Helen danced with this guy that I think was a senior. "Are we talking dropdead gorgeous or what?" she whispered to me during a break. I smiled and nodded yes, but I really didn't see it. He was cute and all that, but he wasn't David.

Walking home, we were feeling the air, the crispness of it. The sky was wide and purple-black, cut with stars. I don't remember what we were talking about. Maybe Maggie. But maybe not. It was the not speaking that drew us into that kiss. When we first crossed the highway and were into the subdivision, we stopped, just standing there, looking out at the sky, the houses and the hills beyond them, and then at each other.

I got lost looking at David. And then we weren't looking anymore. He was kissing me and I was kissing him back. I remember how warm his lips were, how good it felt when he rubbed his cheek on mine, how he touched my hair and my face like he was blind and wanted to know me. I remember how excited I felt when I heard his gasp and knew then he was excited too, how he kissed me again, hungrier then, wanting more. How I never wanted to stop but only to kiss him forever, kiss him soft and hard, light and deep, and kiss him more, more.

When we did stop, I couldn't look at him. He tilted my head up until I had to and there he was, smiling at me. So gently. David was the gentlest human being I ever knew. He ran a finger lightly over my eyebrows and down the side of my face. I was trembling with cold and fever, with what I know is desire. He pulled me closer then and stood with his chin on my hair, breathing me in.

"Livvie." That was all he said. Livvie. I felt a melting thrill run through me like the roll of drums, felt it deep and full. I nuzzled my head into his neck and breathed his warmth.

Later, when we got to my house and it was time for him to go, we looked again and I could see it still — his wanting me. Could he see me wanting him? We both smiled then and said goodbye, the careful, studied goodbye we always said on the street outside my door. And perhaps we looked the same to my mother who was peering out from behind the curtains as she often did, but we were not. We'd moved a step somehow. Kissing like that was more than holding hands.

Because we were taking Mrs. Fulton's class together, we talked about sex as though it was yesterday's news. We'd quizzed each other on reproductive anatomy, the sexual response cycle, on nocturnal emissions and premenstrual syndrome. We could name fourteen sexually transmitted diseases, rattle off the ten most common symptoms of AIDS, and quote the latest statistics on five different methods of birth control. We were good students and Mrs. Fulton was a good teacher, but none of it had anything to do with us. Not really.

Or did it?

At first it was painfully embarrassing to speak or even listen to words like penis, vagina, orgasm. I'd squirm in my chair and wish I was dead and gone from there, wish Mrs. Fulton would quit. But as the term progressed I changed. Maybe all of us in that class did. Mrs. Fulton called it desensitisation. She said that since we were being innundated with words about sex, they would lose some of their power to shock us. And that was true. Her hope was that without the shock and the embarrassment we would be able to consider sex more clearly. Which she hoped meant we would be able to make better decisions. Translated, it meant "Wait." Don't have sex because he says he loves you, don't have sex because you don't know what else to do to show him that you love him, that you care.

I think that's part of what the caring projects were about — finding other ways to show love besides sex. Did we love Maggie? Actually, I think we did. But it was all wrapped up in the love we had for each other. It was something to do with our love, a place to put the energy. We loved Maggie Parker, yes. But we loved each other more.

13

As Thanksgiving grew near and the cool weather continued Maggie seemed better. She pooched out a little in front, just a little, but she said she could feel the baby move and she knew, just *knew* that things were going to be okay. Then she'd knock wood. Sometimes now she could go for two or three days without throwing up. Her bleeding slowed and then stopped. And finally, just after the first frost, the blasting from the highway was finished. Good omens all.

One day she asked what we thought about names. Did we like Abraham for a boy, Sarah for a girl? What did we think about Rosie, short for Roselle, or Walker for a boy?

"Walker's a little strange isn't it?" she said, wrinkling up her nose and giggling. "But I like it anyway. It's a family name. Of course I don't much want to saddle the little thing with something that would cause him grief later on."

I remember then she laughed.

"But hey, who isn't saddled with grief sooner or

later? And this little one, whoever he or she may be, Rosie or Abraham or Walker or Sarah — whoever's in there — has had a hard way to go getting born. He's walked a longer road than most already. I just hope he'll hang on." She broke off and the words hung there for a moment before she continued. "I want to know this little guy. Must be one tough cookie, don't you think?" she asked, smiling at us with maternal pride.

Actually, I rarely thought about the baby. When we'd studied birth defects in Mrs. Fulton's class, I spent some time looking at pictures of babies that came out hurt or sick or not formed right. I thought about it then, a little. And once David and I talked to Marie about what Maggie's symptoms might mean for the baby. But it seems to me it was David who brought it up. He asked Marie how Maggie could stay pregnant when she was bleeding.

"It depends, David," she said. "It depends on whether she's losing part of the placenta or simply some old blood left in the uterus. And you guys know what the placenta is? And the uterus?"

We both nodded.

"Well, bless Mrs. Fulton. If it's the placenta there's a chance the baby won't be properly nourished in the last months. Which may or may not matter. Does she take vitamins?"

Neither one of us knew. We came to Marie on occasion for medical advice which we would then spirit back to Maggie, delivering it as if it was contraband from another world.

"Should she?" David asked. "Take vitamins?"

We were sitting in their kitchen, on those high wooden stools, drinking tea. "Tell her to talk to her doctor about it. It might be a good idea if she can tolerate it."

"Is the baby going to be all right?" David asked her then. He said it real fast, like he hadn't meant to ask that, but it had come out anyway. "Do you think it's going to live?"

Marie studied him, her brown eyes unblinking. "Oh honey, I don't know. Every month she carries, the baby has a better chance of living at birth. But it's all so chancy. And a good deal of it is out of our hands anyway." She looked sad, older than usual somehow. "Some people believe God gives parents handicapped children as a special gift. That may be true. But on the other hand, most miscarriages — which is what it sounds like Mrs. Parker missed by just the slightest chance — most miscarriages are of babies that . . . were . . . they . . . born," she spoke slowly for emphasis, "would be deformed or severely handicapped. So . . . " Her hands spread outward in a gesture of uncertainty. "I really don't know."

One day, Maggie met us at the door waving a letter at us, her face wreathed in smiles. "Look at this!" She was like a kid at Christmas. "It just came. Two thousand dollars! Can you believe it? Sweet day! They paid off. The insurance company. Two thousand dollars!" We'd never seen her like that, so happy.

She and David spent most of that day walking the

property, making estimates about repair costs. David told me later that he'd had to take a big stick with him and beat around on the ground in front of them when they'd gotten close to the basement. But at least she was outside. Mostly, she was too scared even to leave the house for fear of snakes.

I stayed in the kitchen making bread for her from a recipe that Marie said was good for pregnant women. It had lots of eggs in it and milk. I could hear Maggie's voice rising in excitement, full of laughter and lighter than I'd ever heard her before. It seems mingled, at least in memory, with the warm yeasty scent of that baking bread.

When they came in, she was flushed and red-cheeked with cold. She put an arm around me and gave me a little hug. "Oh Livvie, this is wonderful. Isn't it? Look at that crack in the dining room," she said, pulling me to follow. "Maybe there'll be enough money left over to fix it. It would look so pretty in here with some new wallpaper. So nice." She squeezed me and sighed. "Wouldn't it be fine to sit down in here and we could have supper and Dean would like it? Don't you think he would like it?"

It was as much as she had ever said to me about her husband and I wasn't sure how to answer. "I'd say anybody would like it in here, Maggie. It's a pretty room," I answered carefully.

And it was pretty. The windows faced straight into the hill behind the house, into the apple orchard and beyond. That day, the leaves had turned but were not finished dropping, so the view was a framed blaze of colour.

We stayed late that day and were just coming down the steps and onto Bayberry when Mr. Parker drove up. David and I both smiled at him and nodded hello. It seemed certain that when he got up to the house and saw Maggie's face and that cheque for two thousand dollars, even he, Old Sobersides, the beast himself, was bound to smile too. He looked at us with grim slitted eyes, slammed the car door as he always did, and ignoring us, walked up the steps. A little shiver ran through me which David must have felt because he put his arm around me as though to warm me up.

The next day and the day after that, Maggie came to the door in a bathrobe and said she was resting; could we come back later? After that, if either one of us mentioned the repairs or the money she would grow quiet and vague and change the subject.

Neither David nor I could figure it out. Sometimes we tried. "Maybe he's a compulsive gambler and he had to use the money to pay off his debts," I suggested once. David laughed. "Or else he'll get shot or thrown in the river or whatever it is they do with people like that."

"But isn't the money hers?" David asked. From his tone I knew he was thinking about it more seriously than I had been. So I considered.

"I don't know. She said the house was hers, but they're married. Maybe it's common property. How does that work?"

"I'm not sure. We could ask your parents."

"No way."

"I just meant, you know, they're married."

"I know, but no."

David smiled and reached over to tousle my hair.

"Whatever happened, it wasn't good," I said, thinking of Maggie's eyes, the distance in them and the pain.

"No, it's not good," David agreed. "And it's something to do with him. That's what I think."

"He really bugs you, doesn't he? But why? Why does he matter? He's a jerk." (You see, Hirsch, for me, then, that explanation was complete. He was a jerk. Period.)

I heard David sigh and he slowed his step. I slowed too. Finally, he answered. "I think, I think it's because — I don't know if you can understand this, Livvie."

"Try me," I said, feeling hushed inside, as though I were holding my breath. "If you want."

David glanced up at the clouds and back down at our feet. If I remember correctly there was a drizzle that day. "All my life," he glanced at me, "whenever I would meet a man — I've been doing this since I was five — I would always think, What if he were my father? Not that I think every man I meet *could* be my father, that isn't it. Just, what kind of father would he be? Especially, if he were mine."

"Oh, David." I felt sad and put my arm around his waist.

He leaned his cheek to my head. "Does that sound crazy?"

"No. I understand it. I think I do anyway."

"So when I see someone like him, someone I can't fathom, someone I don't even like, it bothers me. I think — " his voice was very soft, and I leaned closer to hear him — "I don't even *know* what I think, Liv, but it bothers me. A lot."

So often the thread we picked at, thinking it was the Parkers, turned out to be ourselves instead. In talking about them we began to unravel each other. Or was it that the thread of who they were, and who we imagined them to be, grew so long that it wound us together, binding us closer and closer? You're the one with perspective, Hirsch. What do you say. Or does it matter?

Maggie stayed skittish about snakes, worse then skittish, afraid. Terrified may not be putting it too strongly. Even when the weather was freezing and David would assure her they were fast asleep somewhere deep in the woods she would shudder and say, "Under the house. That's what I'm scared of. That they're under the house." And then she would mock herself, say, "God, what a fool I am. It's true. Poor Dean, having to put up with a dimwit like me. I know there's nothing to be frightened of, but I am. I'm such an idiot."

"No, you're not, Maggie," David and I would say. "You're scared and that's different."

Phobic is the word Marie used when we told her about it. She sighed and shook her head and said that although Maggie's fear might be irrational, it was real enough. We knew that. There were times I could almost smell her fear; it hung around her like a cloak.

Maggie gained weight, or at least she began really to bulge in the middle. The rest of her, her arms and legs stayed stick thin and her face had a papery white, frightened look that nothing David or I did seemed to ease.

At Thanksgiving, the end of our first term, the end of sex-ed, Mrs. Fulton asked again what we had learned from our caring project. I told her it was hard to quit and she laughed out loud and said, "Oh Olivia, thank you for that."

Instead of a final exam in sex-ed we filled out an evaluation sheet. It was as if Mrs. Fulton were the one being tested. When we were finished she had everyone in the class stand in a big circle and give the person in front a shoulder rub. She said she thought we knew enough to do that now. Whether we knew enough or not, it was fun. Thirty people in a big circle. I heard Helen mutter to David, "If *this* is what she thinks sex is all about, it's no wonder she thinks we should wait." He tilted his head back and laughed, a sound as mellow and warm as the sunshine streaming in. There were giggles and snorts and smiles all around the circle that day. We were happy. Happy.

That was the end of sex-ed. Mrs. Fulton was different after we went on to regular biology. When she wasn't giving automatic A's she was a hell of a hard grader and extremely strict about homework.

14

And then came Christmas. Oh Hirsch, please no. I don't want to go on. I hate this, hate it. Do you hear me? Does it matter? Do you really call this healing? It hurts, damn you. And for what? It's not as if all the telling in the world could undo one minute of it. It's over, gone, done, and none of that can change. Ever. Is this how shrinks get their kicks, wallowing in other people's pain? No, I know that's not fair. Not completely anyway, although I really *don't* understand the point of this. I want it finished. I want to go fast, you want it slow. Christmas. Okay, Christmas.

I studied for a long time what to give David. I wanted it to be perfect, just right. I've never been good at picking out gifts for people. The strain of it, of trying to get it right, depresses me. I got Mom a vase for flowers. Sometimes she uses it so maybe she likes it. For Dad, I got a tie that David and I picked out together. He wears one to work every day so I figured even if he wasn't wild about it, it would come in useful.

For Marie I chose a scarf and David decided on a

record. It had psalms from the Bible set to music and sung by some monks. David and Marie both believed in God and seemed to get comfort from that in a way I never really understood. At this point, I don't expect I ever will. I'm grateful that neither one of them pushed me about religion, or even implied there was anything wrong with me for not having a belief one way or the other. That's the way they were.

For Maggie's present, we eventually settled on a cloth carrier for the baby. We thought it might give her hope, but it was a hard decision. At least we had each other to discuss it with. For days, David and I walked the mall looking at one thing and another, talking it over, laughing, listening to the Christmas Muzak, holding hands. All that time I was thinking, what can I get for you? You, David. What would you like?

My mother says the best gift is one you would want yourself, but I couldn't be sure. Finally, I settled on *A Christmas Memory*, a book by Truman Capote. It had an old faded picture on the front of the author as the very young boy Buddy, standing with his old friend. It didn't seem a very romantic gift, but I loved the story and I thought maybe, maybe David would too.

I also baked him some bread. We'd found out in sex-ed about subliminal advertising — using sexual allusions to sell things. I was afraid he might remember Mrs. Fulton explaining that 'Nothing says lovin' like something from the oven' could be understood on two levels, one of them being that 'oven' was a slang word for vagina. But I also remembered Marie quoting some

French chef that 'Not only is love the most important ingredient in making bread, it is in fact the only ingredient.' And I liked that. As I kneaded that dough I thought of nothing but David, and it was the happiest, lightest loaf I ever baked.

To our total amazement, and I think to Maggie's too, she invited us to a 'little Christmas get-together'. Her husband wanted to have some friends from work over and had told her to invite some other people. David and I were the only 'other people' Maggie knew. I see now how very sad and peculiar that was, but at the time I thought nothing of it.

A few days before the party, David and I climbed up on the hill to gather some wild holly for her to decorate the house with. We walked all the way to where the new cut was being made in the highway. It was a dismal, muddy mess. We could see where trees had been knocked down and left sprawling dead like forgotten corpses. One forlorn looking bulldozer sat there in the freezing rain, sloshed with mud. It was so ugly we turned away and David wondered out loud again what had ever become of that insurance money. But elsewhere we found holly and evergreen branches that Maggie took delight in and arranged, with big red candles, in various corners of the house.

The night of the party David came over to get me at seven o'clock. We were both wearing good clothes and feeling a little nervous. I could smell that he'd shaved, which he only did now and then. I had on a bright green blouse that I was hoping would make my eyes look green too. (It didn't.) Mom of course was there, smiling at us and saying things like "Mind your manners, Livvie" and "You two know better than to drink anything alcoholic even if it's offered." She gave me a box of bath powder to take to Maggie. The two of them had never met.

David and I knew the party was already in full swing from the cars parked at the bottom of Bayberry. We could hear music coming from the house and it was all lit up. Maggie answered the door looking really beautiful. Her thick, dark hair was pinned up but there were little curly tendrils falling down. She wore a maternity dress made from some satiny black material and she was smiling.

"I'm so glad you're here," she said, pulling us in. "Let me see if I can introduce you." We followed her into the living room, which seemed packed with people and music.

"Dean, Dean," she said to Mr. Parker. "This is David and Livvie."

Mr. Parker looked at us for a brief moment and nodded. Nothing more.

The other people there, the ones whose names Maggie could remember, shook hands with us and made small talk. Mr. Parker, it turned out, worked for a radio station. One of the people there was a disc jockey that my mother listened to every morning. We found out Mr. Parker wrote commercials. For some reason it surprised me that he should have a job like that. David and I had both wondered what he did, although we'd never asked Maggie, but we'd assumed it was something gruesome and strange, *not* writing commercials.

Maggie brought us big mugs of cinnamon-spiced cranberry tea. Mr. Parker was busy filling up people's drinks from a bar they'd set up in the dining room. I saw him smiling and talking to people so I knew he was capable, but the most David or I ever got was that nod. He ignored us. Some man, I forget his name, said, "This is an incredible house, Dean. It's like something from another time."

A woman who had the longest, blondest, shiniest hair I've ever seen chimed in. "I know exactly what you mean. It's like an old dinosaur perched up here on its hill, looking down at the suburbs. If you could shut out the rest of it, you could really imagine you were living in the last century."

She smiled at Mr. Parker and he handed her a drink, taking a long time to do it, smiling back.

In the living room the radio was turned up so loud it was difficult to talk. Mostly, I didn't need to talk since hardly anyone talked to me. I felt awkwardly young and out of place. David, however, got immediately into a conversation with some man about a scandal going on just then in state government. I was amazed that he knew so much about it. It was not a subject we had ever discussed together and I felt shy and a little sad to realise that he had thoughts we'd never shared.

Maggie seemed to be having a good time. Several times, I saw her pat her belly, and I wondered if the baby was kicking in time to the music. Yellow-grey cigarette smoke fanned up from the lamps and I saw her wave some away from her face when she was talking to the woman with the long hair. It made me angry that the lady was so dumb as to blow smoke in a pregnant woman's face. Maggie had made all kind-of little snacks to eat and I nibbled at some as carefully as I could, certain I would spill something and embarrass myself.

I was talking to Maggie, saying something stupid but polite like "This is a great dip," when I realised that she wasn't listening. Her face had gone suddenly ashen and strange. Horror-stricken may be the word. I followed her gaze and saw the blonde lady sitting on Mr. Parker's lap. He was laughing at something she said and patting her thigh. She was feeding him a little cracker and sort of nuzzling her breasts up toward his face. She was laughing too.

Nobody else acted like there was anything unusual about it, which made the whole scene even weirder. Maggie looked so small, so big-eyed, so devastated. I reached for her hand and without thinking pulled her out of the room and into the kitchen. David was in there, still talking to that same man. Some other people were there too. David saw me and waved me over.

"Hey, Livvie. You doing okay?" he said in a soft voice.

"I don't think so, David," I answered, matching his tone. He gave me a puzzled look and I nodded my head toward the living room. He gave me a little squeeze on the back of my neck and excused himself.

Maggie stood in front of the refrigerator with the door open, staring. I touched her back and she flinched.

"Oh, I'm sorry, Livvie. It's you. I'll be back in a minute." And she walked off. I shut the refrigerator door and watched her. She looked unsteady. David came back in and gave me a look that meant it was time to go.

"What about saying goodbye?" I asked him.

"It's okay. I think we should get out of here."

And so we did. Without a word to either one of the Parkers and only the briefest goodbye to the man David had been talking to, we found our coats and were gone. Outside, the air felt stingingly cold but clean. I took several deep breaths trying to rinse from myself some scum I felt clinging inside me. Mr. Parker and that woman.

"So you saw?" I asked as we got to the bottom step. The words came firing out. I felt angry, not at David exactly, but a little at him too. I don't know why.

"Yeah. I saw," he said. "Poor Maggie."

Without knowing I was going to, I burst into tears. Big, painful sobbing heaves kept coming up from my stomach and into my chest and I cried just as hard as I could. We had passed my house and were walking, just walking the streets as we did so often. I didn't even try to quit crying, I wanted to cry. We walked and I cried and David put his arm around me and didn't say another word.

When I finally finished, I pulled a Kleenex out of my pocket and wiped my eyes and my nose. I felt empty, tired. We walked back to the house and before he left David pulled me close to his chest and whispered hoarsely, "I love you, Livvie." That was the first time he'd ever said that. "I would never do that to you. Never. I promise." He held me so tightly I could neither speak nor breathe nor think and then he ran off into the night and, dazed, I went to bed.

15

The next morning I woke with a fever of 103. I spent the next few days, including Christmas, asleep — unconscious practically. David called but Mom wouldn't let anyone up to see me.

Through fever and pain I had a recurring dream that Dean Parker was kissing me. I would fight him off but I could smell his foul breath on my face, taste the drool from his lips, see his ugly black eyes laughing, feel his hands clutching at my arms, my breasts. I would wake moaning and thrashing, drenched in my own sweat, fighting nothing more than covers, and sink, shaking, into the same dream again. And again.

When the fever finally broke I was able to sit up in bed, but I was dizzy and had a hard time focusing on what was going on around me. Mom and Dad would sit with me and talk, but when they were gone I couldn't remember what had been said.

By the time David came over to visit it was almost New Year's. Mom brought him up to my room. I felt shy, for he'd never been in my room, never seen me in bed. I remember glancing at my dresser and seeing my deodorant, my hairbrush, my cologne, and thinking, Now he'll know all my secrets. Mom brought us tea and leftover Christmas cookies on a tray, and smiling, but not closing the door, left us alone. David pulled my desk chair up to the bed and sat there looking at me with the same doctorly bedside expression I'd seen him use on Maggie.

"You had us pretty worried there, Liv. Are you better?" He took one of my hands in both of his and I sat there looking at it as it lay on the white coverlet. David's hands were big; he could palm a basketball easily. He had long, rough fingers and some of his nails were bitten. For a while neither of us said any more.

"Have you been to see Maggie?" I asked at last, rousing myself to speak of what lay between us.

"No." He shook his head and I felt him squeeze my hand. "In fact, they've gone away for the week. Relatives, according to Mrs. Bertman."

We both laughed. How Mrs. Bertman kept up with the movements of people in the neighbourhood was a mystery to us, but her information had always proved reliable. We dismissed both the Parkers with that laugh. Gone. Good. I didn't want to think about it.

David and I exchanged presents. Mom had already given him the bread I'd baked. He'd come by on Christmas day, but I'd been too ill to see him. Sadly, I watched him unwrap the book. I was certain I'd made a bad choice, but there was nothing else to do for it by then. He looked at it a long time and then leaned over and kissed me very gently, thank you, on the forehead.

"You're so pale, Livvie. I want you to get better."

"I am better," I told him, but I think we were both unconvinced.

He brought out a small box wrapped in red tissue paper. Inside, on a bed of cotton, lay a small gold medallion on a thin gold chain. Imprinted on it was the figure of a man and some Latin words.

"It's Saint Jude," David said. "He's the patron saint of impossible causes."

I held it up to the light and watched it glint and turn. "Thank you."

"I know you're not Catholic. I'm not either — as you know. But somehow . . . it just seemed like something you might like." He looked embarrassed, slightly flushed.

"I do like it, David," I said truthfully. "But does this mean you think I'm an impossible cause?" I was trying to kid him out of his discomfort.

"Oh Livvie," he said very softly. "You're the most possible cause of all." I felt a thrill of warm, healing light tingle through me. "I really can't explain why I thought it suited you," he continued, looking down. "I just did. I feel a little dumb giving it to you, but I wanted you to have it. To have it be from me."

"I like it a lot, David. Help me put it on."

I swept my hair up and David leaned over and fastened it behind my neck. The medal hung cold for a moment on my chest, but soon I could feel it heating up, a warm spot near my heart. Saint Jude.

David kissed me then on the mouth and smoothed my hair with his hands. He tasted of toothpaste. I probably did too. "I love you, Livvie. I mean that."

And I told him at last what had been aching in me for months. "I love you too, David. I love you too."

He moved over onto the bed and held me in his arms. I felt my blood racing and for a moment it was hard to catch my breath. When he got up we looked away from each other not in shame exactly, but not unlike that either. I felt my cheeks burning, but now not with fever. Just as he was almost out the door we caught each other's eyes. We both started grinning. After he left, I lay in bed smiling to myself for a long, long time.

Mrs. Fulton often said love was something you could never prove, not with sex or in any way at all. It could never be demanded or measured. She said it was a gift that came unearned, undeserved even. A gift. And Mrs. Fulton was right. But what she never did say, never told us at all, was how love wanted sex. Not for proof, but for love itself, for more. At least, so it was with us.

Speaking those words — I love you — speaking them out loud, made us both a little crazy. Hot. Call it what you will. Once I was better we continued as before, hands in each other's pockets, heads together, walking the winter streets. But things had changed. Kissing was harder and longer and almost impossible to stop. When he pulled me to him I could feel him shaking. There was a roughness to him as if he were angry, but I knew it wasn't anger at all.

I began to want David in a way that frightened me, as if my skin was melting, as if I was drowning for real and the only thing I could breathe, the only thing that could save me was more of him. Sex — yes Mrs. Fulton, I wanted to have sex with him, but that was only part of it. I wanted to marry him, have babies with him, grow old together. I wanted everything a person wants. Everything.

16

School started. David and I walked home together as usual that first day back. Without discussing it, we turned down Bayberry, walked past my house and up the steps to Maggie's. We had not spoken of the Christmas party at all. I suppose neither one of us knew quite what to say.

It took a long time for Maggie to open the door and when she did I was startled by the change in her appearance. Her hair was uncombed and her right arm lay in a sling. She looked bad — paler than usual, and very, very tired. She stood there in the doorway letting the cold air blow into the house, gazing at us vacantly. I think she didn't know us right away.

"Maggie?" David said tentatively. "May we come in? Are you okay? What happened to your arm?"

Finally she stirred. "Oh. Hi. Yes." She stood aside and let us in. Her voice sounded strange, hoarse and low, as if she hadn't spoken for a long time, yet thin, as though she were disappearing or speaking to us from far away.

We followed her into the living room. I felt uneasy. There were papers and magazines strewn about, dirty glasses on the coffee table, a coat and some sweaters on the couch.

"We heard you went away to visit relatives over Christmas," I said. "Did you have a good time?" Whatever Maggie had been having it was not a good time, but I was at a loss for what else to say. She stared at me for a moment and nodded her head.

"So what *did* happen to your arm?" David persisted.

"Oh. That." She looked down at her sling. "I'm so stupid. I really am." She bent her curly brown head toward her hurt arm and stared at it. I saw that her hair was thinning.

David looked up suddenly toward the ceiling and then out the window to the sky beyond. I think he was praying.

"I wrenched it," she continued slowly. "It's not bad."

We sat there in silence. None of us alluded to the last time we'd seen each other — to the Christmas party. To the fact that her husband had been holding another woman on his lap, feeding her crackers and cheese. I wish we had. I wish we'd known of something to say that would have helped.

David broke the silence first. "So Maggie, how's the baby doing? How are you feeling? Your time is getting pretty close, isn't it?"

"Is it?" she asked. A sudden shiver of fear slid through me.

"Maggie." David kept on her. "We'd be happy to help. What can we do? Maybe you want to go to bed and rest?"

"Go to bed?" she asked.

"Wouldn't you like to rest? You look tired."

"Rest? Yes. I'd like that." She made no move. "What are we talking about?" she asked us then, looking first at David and then at me.

I began to feel really afraid. "We could straighten up in here, couldn't we?" I said taking my cue from David who was nodding at me. "How about it? I could get supper started for you."

"Maggie," David said. He leaned right up in her face and didn't go on until she was looking at him. "What's wrong?"

"David?" she said. "Is that you?"

"Yes, it is. And Livvie's here too. We want to help."

"David," she said and her voice was high and animated for the first time, "David, there's a hole in the floor in the bathroom. I think the snakes can get in through there. It's not big, but they don't need a big hole, do they?" Her eyes were huge blue and black puddles. She looked so afraid. So horribly frightened, and frail.

David didn't remind her it was the middle of winter. He didn't argue or try to reason with her at all. "I'll fix that hole for you. Would you like that?" he asked.

"Yes. I would. Will you cover it? Will you cover it tight?"

"You got it, Maggie. It's as good as fixed right now.

Why don't you go get in bed and Livvie and I will get on it right away. Okay?"

She nodded. David and I exchanged a look. I got up and took her uninjured arm, which was thinner than ever, and led her, like a child, to bed. I heard David go into the kitchen and knew he was getting the tool box.

The bedroom was a mess. There were clothes all over the floor, hanging on chairs, thrown over the dresser and the bed itself, which was a tangle of sheets and blankets. Maggie stood dumbly, watching me pick things up and smooth out the covers for her. I cleared away the bed and motioned for her to come lie down. For a moment I felt like my mother; she had done the very same for me a few weeks before when I was the sick one.

Maggie wasn't wearing any shoes, just these big, black, thick, woollen socks, so she lay right down and I covered her up, smothing first the sheets, then the blanket, and patting down the quilt on top. She curled up on her left side, resting her bent, hurt right arm in front of her body. I saw her left hand pat her abdomen which was swollen under a bright red maternity dress. If she'd been slow to show her pregnancy at first that was over now. She looked very pregnant in the middle but like sticks and bones everywhere else. I tucked her in. I almost bent down and kissed her, that's how I was feeling, but she turned first and looked at me.

"Olivia, I do thank you. I may be out of my mind. That may be true, but either way I thank you." She looked me directly in the eye.

"I don't think you're out of your mind, Maggie," I said. Actually, I wasn't sure.

"No? Well, good. But you don't know."

And what would I say if I could talk to her now? Would I tell her what I do know about losing your mind, what I have learned?

David did fix the hole in the bathroom that day. He nailed a tin can lid down and tacked over a piece of old green carpet he found out in their shed. He said they must have been losing a lot of heat through that hole. What a practical thought. Maggie had the ingredients for a tuna casserole on her shelves and I had just learned how to make it that week in Home Ec., so I put it together for her and left it wrapped on the kitchen table. Then I did the dishes and straightened chairs and wiped down counters in the kitchen.

We thought about cleaning up the living room a little, but we were both anxious to get out of there. It felt creepy. I can't explain it much more than that — creepy, weird, scary.

Instead of walking down the steps and back to my house David said he wanted to go to the highway. So we walked up the hill, through the orchard and up to the deserted place where the road was half finished, half frozen in time. The bulldozer was still there and David took a rag out of his coat and brushed off the little bit of snow that was in it. We sat in there, inside the big shovel of that dozer, sheltered from the wind, watching the highway.

At first we talked about Maggie. Neither one of us

knew what to do about it beyond what we were doing — making ourselves useful and caring. "What do you think is wrong, Liv?" David asked me.

"I don't know. What do you think?"

"I don't know either." Back and forth like that we went, neither one of us making much sense, just talking, watching the cars, sitting close for warmth and comfort.

We cared about Maggie, maybe more than ever, but what was wrong with her had evidently gone beyond what we could fix. From this distance, it is easy, sickeningly easy to see what we might have done to help. We could have told someone, Marie, Mrs. Fulton, *someone*, what was going on. We could have told about the Christmas party, but we didn't. The worse things got, the more we kept it to ourselves.

And then we stopped talking about Maggie. There was no point to it anymore. Instead we talked about each other. David traced the line of my eyebrows with his finger. "Your eyes give you away," he said.

"How so?"

"I advise you not to play poker, Liv. It could cost you a lot of money."

"David, what are you talking about?" I sensed a joke coming, something.

"I love you too, buddy," he told me then, not joking. Not joking at all. "You show it so plainly, you ought to know that I love you too. In case it doesn't show on my face the way it does on yours. In case you wonder sometimes, What's he thinking? What does he feel about me? You should know that I love you too."

We finally got cold and walked back down the hill, through the orchard, and out the Parkers' side yard. We'd just started down the first flight of steps to Bayberry when Mr. Parker started up. All three of us froze. Then he kept coming and David and I stood aside to let him pass. He didn't look at us, but brushed by and said in a low, threatening growl, "You kids stay the hell away from here." I felt David's arm stiffen around my shoulders, but neither of us said anything.

We went anyway the next day, but Maggie shook her head at us from a crack in the door and said she was sleeping. The day after that we called her on the phone. We'd never done that before, and had to call information to get the number. Maggie said she didn't want any company, that she was feeling 'poorly' and wanted to rest. And it went on like that for days, until one day we realised that three weeks had passed and we hadn't seen her.

So January was ours. Without Maggie. We spent a lot of the time we'd been using up at her house doing homework. After Mrs. Fulton finished with sex education she tore into that biology book with something like a vengeance. She covered whole chapters of stuff that I only barely understood and kept going. It was way too fast and too much for me. But David kept up or even ahead and helped me along. In turn, I helped him with essays and book reports for English. Neither one of us really minded homework, and doing it together was an extra bonus.

Biology came easy to David. He mentioned several times that maybe he would be a doctor and what did I think. Always he was asking me, "What do you think, Liv?" Like my opinion mattered. What I thought was that he'd be a natural for it, and I told him that, too. David had healing in him.

We'd meet at the lockers every day after school. "Where to?" David would ask, even after it got to be a joke.

"Someplace warm."

"Your house is closest."

"Not my house."

"It's warm. And if I know your mother, she'll make us hot chocolate."

"Hot chocolate has its price."

David thought this was funny. "What are you worried about?"

"I'm not worried, I'd just rather go anywhere else. She gets on my nerves."

"I don't see why. Your mom's okay."

"She's okay. I'm not saying she's not, but she's *too* interested, if you know what I mean. I feel like she's hovering just above my shoulder, pecking at me with her questions. Honestly, don't you get that feeling?"

"I don't know. I guess I think she's a little lonely, maybe. Or bored. But she's okay."

"She's wasting herself selling Avon."

"You ever mentioned that to her?"

"Yeah, and forget it. She gets totally hyper if I bring up anything that smells even slightly of women's liberation. But I still think she'd be happier doing something else."

"I'd say you'd be happier, for sure," he said, smiling his cock-eyed smile.

"Yeah, something that took her out of the house."

"Every day."

"At least till six." We both laughed, understanding each other completely. How good to have someplace we could be alone.

Sometimes we went to the library, which was a very long walk. Even for us. Usually we went to his house and worked in the kitchen. Marie was often there, in and out, but I didn't mind her the way I did my own mother. David didn't mind it at either house, but I had a definite preference for his. Marie left us alone.

Marie left us alone, but now I wish she hadn't. If anyone could have helped us, helped Maggie, helped at all, it would have been Marie. But she never interfered, never once butted in. She wasn't intrusive and I liked her for that at the time. But now there are times when I blame her, when I think she should have done something, stopped us, changed it. I go around and around but it doesn't help. It's over now.

Somedays we'd walk down to the mall instead of straight home. It was warm in there, and we'd get something to eat and just hang out. I liked it. There were always kids from school hanging out too, and although I never spent much time with anybody in particular except David, I liked being known, included by his friends. And I loved being David's girl. Helen once told me she always knew David would go for someone different, an outsider. She said it approvingly, said we made sense. And we did.

Maybe because we weren't seeing Maggie there wasn't anything else to do with that excess of love, of energy. Maybe we would have had the idea anyway, I don't know. But it came to us both that we wanted to make love. Both. There were days I could hardly get near him without feeling so turned on it was hard to keep my hands off him. He was the same. It seems we were always looking at each other and I could read it as plainly in his eyes as I guess he could in mine.

And then one day we talked about it. Was there anything we couldn't talk about? We'd been kissing, outside as usual, and it was freezing cold. My nose was numb and he kept blowing on it to warm it up. There were low, grey storm clouds racing across the night sky.

"I want to make love to you, Livvie," he whispered, kissing the tip of my nose. "I want to do it and do it right." I shut my eyes and he kissed the lids. "I'm not going to let anything hurt you. I promise you that."

"I want to, David," I told him. My voice was husky and cracking. "I want it too."

"We'll have to figure out birth control," he said drawing back and smiling at me, his brown eyes crinkling at the corners. "But we've been educated, right? We ought to be able to handle it. Did you keep your notes on birth control?"

I laughed. "Yes. I did, did you?"

"You better believe I saved them, girl. I might even get them laminated, hang them on the wall."

He kissed me fast and hard then six, eight, a dozen times on the lips, my cheeks, my nose, my eyes. We were both laughing and suddenly it started to snow. The wind died down and for a moment there was only the sound of us laughing. Everything else was quiet, snowbound, dark. The houses looked empty as if David and I had the night to ourselves.

I caught my breath. "But seriously, David, what do we do? Go to Planned Parenthood?"

"I guess. Or the health department. Seems like she said the health department did birth control too. And I can use condoms, for my part." There were big soft white flakes in his hair, on his lashes.

"If we don't go in soon," I said and my teeth chattered from excitement as much as cold, "we'll be in the hospital with pneumonia."

"Great idea, Livvie." David wrapped his long arms around me and hugged me hard, lifting me briefly off my feet. "You're a diabolical genius. We can ask about birth control while they're listening to our lungs and taking our blood pressure. What a devious mind you've got. I love it." He hugged me once more and we parted that night laughing.

We never did call Planned Parenthood or the health department and we didn't get pneumonia. None of that happened. Instead, Maggie had her baby. We saw her going off to the hospital. It was January thirtieth at six o'clock in the evening. Mr. Parker was helping her down the steps. David and I were just turning the corner into Bayberry, on the way to my house. Maggie waved and we ran to them.

"This is it!" she said, smiling at us with real excitement. "This baby's coming out of here for sure. Wish me luck, you two." She was flushed and happy, her blue eyes were sparkling. She looked beautiful and seemed well, really well, at last.

On impulse I reached out and hugged her. "Oh Maggie, the best of luck," I said. "You'll do great. I can't wait to see the baby." Suddenly that was true.

"Everything's going to be okay," she whispered into my neck. "You just wait and see. I feel it. I know it. It's all going to be okay."

And I believed her.

Even Mr. Parker seemed different just then. He didn't exactly smile at us, but he didn't scowl either. He looked a little dazed. She had a contraction, a labour pain, just as she was getting into the car. I saw her bend her head in concentration, her forehead screwed up. Mr. Parker stood holding the car door for her. She took slow, deep breaths and gingerly lowered herself onto the front seat. Quickly, he raced around and got in on the other side.

"Good luck," David called to them as they pulled out, and Mr. Parker actually said, "Thanks."

THE END

17

We saw Maggie for the last time a week later. Mrs. Bertman told us that she'd come home, and that the baby was a boy. Healthy. It was eleven o'clock on a Saturday morning and we knew, from watching the house, that Mr. Parker had just driven off. We decided to go to see her. We didn't want to wait until Monday.

I'd spent that morning making beef-neck soup from a recipe Marie had given me. According to her it was supposed to make a mother's milk plentiful, and Maggie had mentioned that she wanted to breast-feed the baby. David carried the jar for me up the steep steps to the house. They were icy that day. We stood on the porch, ringing the bell and knocking on the door. It was a cold grey morning with a sharp gusty wind. We both stamped our feet to keep warm.

From inside we could hear the high angry wail of a baby. David turned the handle and the door opened. "Maggie?" he called, sticking his head in. I remember so well the look on his face as he turned to me. Alarm, concern. Not panic. "Maggie?" he called again and taking my hand, pulled me inside.

We heard her moan.

We moved toward that sound, upstairs towards their bedroom and then, holding each other's hand, we were there. The smell hit me before anything else. The air was foul with the odours of human waste — faeces and urine and blood and sour milk. In the bed lay Maggie, distorted, twisted, groaning with pain, and crying.

"Help me, God," she sobbed over and over, "help me." Next to her lay the baby, squalling too, a red wrinkled bundle. Maggie seemed unaware of us all.

Had I been there alone I probably would have run, run for help, I suppose, but at least run. But David was there and together we knew what to do. We thought we could handle it.

We went to them. I picked up the baby and he quieted for a moment. David put his hand on Maggie's forehead and she opened her eyes, still moaning, and looked at him. Her lips were cracked and dry, and there was blood at one corner of the mouth. She cried out, "I've shit the bed," and dissolved again into tears.

"That's okay," David said soothingly. "That's nothing." He talked to her in a low calming voice, stroking her forehead. To me, he said, "She's got a fever."

I put the baby in his arms. I remember how, even then, in the midst of it all, we handled that little boy so carefully, making sure to hold his head steady and be gentle. "You change him and I'll help here," I told David. We worked as a team, understanding exactly what had to be done even without words. He left the room and I pulled back the covers.

Maggie lay in a soiled flannel nightgown on sheets that were both wet and brown from where she'd voided. At one point I was afraid I was going to gag but didn't. Her pain was greater than her mess, and it was to the pain I was responding. By putting my arms on her shoulders I was able to stop her from thrashing around. I helped her sit up, and then to stand.

She was shaking hard and still crying. "It's okay, Maggie," I kept telling her. "We're here. We're going to help you. It's okay," I crooned.

I helped her out of the nightgown very slowly, first pulling her arms out and then drawing the nightgown carefully over her head. What I saw stunned me. She was covered with bruises. Everywhere. Some were old and greenish yellow. Some, most, were fairly fresh, black and ugly blue. Two places on her arms were raw red and still swelling.

"He's beating you," I gasped. "Maggie, he's beating you."

She didn't meet my eyes, but stood there trembling and naked except for her bloody, brown-stained underpants. I helped her remove them and found a clean sheet on the dresser to wrap her in. There was a rocking chair by the window and I led her to it and helped her sit down.

"No, he's not," she said at last, in a tiny voice. "It

only looks that way. It's my own fault. It's all my fault."

I didn't know what to say. Looking at her swollen, tear-stained face, her matted hair, I felt a wave of intense pity sweep through me, but there was revulsion in it too. Maybe there is always revulsion in pity, I'm not sure. She seemed far younger than I. I became businesslike and certain.

"Let's get you in some clean clothes and get out of here, Maggie. You can't stay. I'll get you a washcloth."

"You don't understand, Olivia."

"What don't I understand?" I snapped at her. "That you're covered with bruises? Didn't they see them in the hospital? What did they say?"

"Most of these weren't there," she said.

"This has happened since you've been home?" I asked. I was incredulous, furious, appalled.

"You don't understand," she repeated. "A husband has his rights. You're too young to understand."

"Rights? Young? Nobody has the right to do this to you. *Nobody*. Do you hear me?"

She nodded and began to cry again. I went into the bathroom to get a wet washcloth. David was walking back and forth in the nursery with the baby on his shoulder.

"She's covered with bruises, David." I could hear my voice coming out as a shout but I couldn't lower it. "Call Marie. Do something. He's *beating* her for Godsake. We've got to get her out of here. Now."

"Oh God," he said quietly. "Has it been that all along and we didn't know it?"

"I don't know," I said, my voice still loud. I couldn't control it.

"I'll get the baby dressed," he said.

I stormed past him into the bathroom where I turned on the faucets, hot and cold, full blast. All I felt then was anger.

I persuaded Maggie to get dressed. I have never, before or since, been so sure of myself. I think she obeyed me because I had no doubt, none, that there was anything else to do but get her and the baby out of there. Right away.

I didn't think about where she would go. My house was closest, but it was Marie I wanted. Marie would know what to do with her, how to make it better. I was sure of that. Perhaps I'd known that for a long time. But David and I had never asked for help, never asked for anything beyond recipes and medical advice. Always, we wanted to handle it ourselves. Maggie was ours.

I helped her put on boots and found her coat. She was totally passive now, quiet. David had wrapped the baby in a quilt and we headed, the four of us, out the side door. David took the lead negotiating the icy spots. Halfway down the walk at the side of the house he turned suddenly, stopped and looked at me. "He's home, Liv." I knew who he meant. "Keep them here. I'll go back in and get him into the house. You wait till he's inside, then take them straight to your mother's."

I nodded in agreement with this plan. I nodded yes, Hirsch. We even smiled at each other ever so slightly before he turned to go back inside. We were partners. I admired again David's ability to stay calm under pressure. Holding Maggie's arm firmly, I stood close to her. Her eyes were wide now with panic, but I looked at her sternly and whispered, "Be quiet." She held her baby close and we sheltered him from the wind. David went back into the house through the side door, through the kitchen.

I waited until I heard him open the front door and call out, "Hey Mr. Parker, that's a fine looking baby you have." I knew he was trying to draw him up to the porch, away from us. I couldn't hear Mr. Parker make any reply, but I heard the sound of his boots going slowly up the slick front steps.

I waited a few more seconds and then motioned, pulling Maggie to come on. She stiffened and looked at me in horror as though suddenly waking up from a dream. "No, Livvie. Stop him. It's not safe." Her eyes were darting and wild.

"Come on," I pulled her again. "We have to get you and the baby out of here. David's okay."

That's what I said. David's okay.

But just then the voices were raised; I heard Dean Parker shout but I couldn't make out the words. I didn't need to. I knew then that Maggie had spoken the truth. Sliding on the ice, I ran down the walk around the side of the house, until I was standing directly at the bottom of the front steps.

I saw David backing away from Mr. Parker, up on the porch. He held his hands in front of him, palms upward. Mr. Parker was poking him hard in the chest with his finger, pushing him back, back.

"What are you kids doing here? Get out, you hear me?" Mr. Parker was yelling, poking him harder and harder, pushing him back.

"David," I screamed. Oh David.

I saw him stagger, lose his balance, watched his arms fling out grasping nothing, a last, useless, graceless, desperate attempt to save himself. I heard him cry out and watched him fall.

David fell forever — boots thrown up from the icy stairs, head down, eyes wide, coming to me.

18

David's neck snapped. He died instantly. People say there could be some comfort in that, but I take none. I saw his face and I know he died scared. It is something I cannot bear. I took my last look of him there as he landed at my feet — broken, dead — I took that sight into seven months of darkness. But when I opened my eyes I could see him still. I see again and again the slow ugly arc his body made, see the sun catch the light from the ice as his boot slipped on that tilted top step; I see his eyes wide open in surprise, in panic, his mouth an O. I am stuck here watching him die.

And I am the only one left.

All that happened next happened without me. You know it better than I, Hirsch. I've heard you recite the list of facts in your low, patient voice. Facts, as if I care. As if they matter. Neighbours came. Police. An ambulance. I was taken to the hospital, David to the morgue. Questions were asked and Mr. Parker was arrested. There was even a trial of sorts, although witnesses for the prosecution were hard to come by. Mrs. Fulton was there and Marie, of course. But what did they know? What was there to know? David and I kept so much to ourselves, and even we didn't know, until it was over, what we were up against.

Maggie never said a word. Somehow that doesn't surprise me. The law you told me about, Hirsch — the one that doesn't allow spouses to be forced to testify against each other? It wasn't the law that kept Maggie quiet. Even if they forced her, I don't think she could have talked. I don't even think it was fear, or not just fear, although God knows she must have been more scared than ever. It was something else, something I don't understand entirely and don't really want to understand. She could never stand up to him, even in her mind. She always thought she was to blame.

The courts called David's death a reckless homicide. Dean Parker was sentenced to one year and served four months. Two more months on probation, isn't that what you said? And now he's a free man. Do I have my facts straight yet? Had I been there the sentence might have been stiffer. He was a violent man, *is* a violent man. And he's out there somewhere, walking around, doubtless holding a job, living a life. But I wasn't there. I was here, blind and speechless and gone. They let him go. If I think about it long enough I will go crazy for sure.

Maggie took the baby and went away, I don't know where. No one does. She left right after the trial and nobody has heard from her since. I only hope she left him. She owes that much to David. But who knows?

Marie moved away. Someone else lives in their house now on Ashwood. She came to see me before she left, but it was during the time I was insensible. I have no memory of it. Instead I have the note she left telling me that David's body had been cremated. She wrote:

Olivia my dear,

I am taking David's ashes up to Cincinnati. I thought I might put them in the river. As you know, he was born there. I don't know what else to do. Perhaps he would like that? I hope so.

For myself, I am going away to a retreat run by our church. It is far away from here, and something like a convent. I don't expect to return. I need to talk with God. Perhaps He can help me. For what it's worth, you are in my prayers.

Get well, Olivia. Live. Please. They say that only the good die young so be bad enough to live a long time. David loved you, dear. You made him happy. Thank you for that.

Marie

I don't know how she can stand to talk to God. I couldn't. Who is God to arrange a world where David dies and Mr. Parker walks the streets? What is His problem? Hirsch says if we could understand the ways of God we would be God, not human. Well, I know I am not God.

We had a woman up here who thought she was the Queen of England. Everyone, even the nurses and the doctors, called her Yer Majesty. She was very old, thin, white-haired, and rather elegant somehow although it wasn't her clothes. It was something else, something inside her. She held a formal tea in her room every afternoon at four o'clock. The tea and scones, the cups and saucers, the silver teapot — they were all imaginary, but no one ever mentioned it. That would have been impolite and everyone was always on their best behaviour for her. She expected it. Yer Majesty taught me how to curtsey. Said it was the proper way to greet a queen. Should curtseying ever come in handy, I'll have her to thank.

Unfortunately, they took her off to State. She wasn't getting better. What was wrong with Yer Majesty is called a 'delusion psychosis'. Whatever is wrong with me is not that. If anything, I suffer from a 'lack-of-delusion psychosis'.

Hirsch, you say there is not one true love for each of us. According to you, there are hundreds of people we could love, dozens at least. And you may be right, but I don't care. You never knew David. Never knew him and never will. No words I can write will do him justice, nothing at all can bring him back. So what do you know?

David died but I've got all the symptoms. I am deeply cold and slow and numb. I cannot see how to go on from here. Or why. I miss him so much.

The nurse came in just now to give me my pill. It is noon, time to eat. It's just as well. There is nothing else to say. That's it, Hirsch, from beginning to end. Slowly.

O

EPILOGUE

It is now almost midnight. I squirrelled the sleeping pill they gave me tonight in my cheek and swallowed only water. I wanted to stay up and finish this, Hirsch. I thought I was done but I was wrong.

Mrs. Fulton came to see me this afternoon. She stood in the doorway of my room. I don't know how long she was there. I was looking out the window at the flat, grey February sky, doing what I often do — nothing. She cleared her throat and I turned around. I was surprised to see her.

"May I come in, Olivia?" she asked. I nodded yes. She sat on the daybed. We looked at each other. She looked much the same — thin, pointy faced, green-eyed. "I miss you," she said. "Does that sound funny? I do."

I said nothing.

"Your doctor tells me you are better. I wanted to come before, but he said there was no point."

"No."

"Are you better?" she asked.

I stared at her and she looked down.

"I think about you so much, I worry about you. It's February again. I guess you know." She stared out the window, but there are no trees for her to look at up here on the ninth floor, only sky. She looked at me again. "And then yesterday I had the thought, just out of the blue, 'Olivia's not the one who died. I could go see her.' I hope you don't mind."

"No, I don't." The words came out like glue but they said what I meant.

She cleared her throat again. "What I really came to say is . . . I'm sorry, Olivia. Horribly sorry. Surviving is not a happy thing to do. Those of us who are left have all the time to think of what we did wrong. What we didn't do right." She began to cry. I saw the tears well up in her eyes just before she squeezed them shut. "I feel so responsible for it all, so guilty. I'm sorry. I needed to say it. Say it to you. I'm sorry."

Perhaps I am wrong. Perhaps I am not the only one left.

She sat there crying for a few minutes. I sat there with her, waiting. She pulled a handkerchief out of her purse and stabbed at her eyes, her red pointy nose.

"I should have known," she said finally. "I should have stopped you. I knew there was something wrong. Any man who puts signs up to keep people away — I should have stopped you, but I didn't. I let you both go on, it was my assignment in the first place. Care about someone. What was I thinking of?"

"We wanted to."

"Oh, I know you did." Her voice was throaty and hoarse. "I saw how much fun it was for both of you. And I thought maybe it would be okay. I wasn't thinking. But I should have known. I knew from what you told me that that woman needed help but . . ." she began to cry again.

"But what?" I asked at last.

"But you and David were *not* the ones to do it. That's the part I didn't know, but I should have. You were in over your heads. That man was sick, the woman too in a different way. You were playing with fire and *I didn't stop you.*"

Her shout filled the room, filled my head. For a few moments I felt dizzy and strange as though I were disconnecting from myself, coming apart. And then, as though he were there beside me, I knew suddenly and quite clearly what David would say. What he would want *me* to say to help her.

"Mrs. Fulton." My voice came out strong. She looked at me. "The blame is not yours. Dean Parker killed David, not you. Not even me. And I was there and agreed to it all. It was Mr. Parker. Don't blame yourself for this."

She stared at me, her green eyes wide open. "Do you believe that?" she asked in a whisper.

"Yes. I know it." And I did. Suddenly I did. "You did the best you could. So did I. So did David. Even Maggie, in her way. The blaming is of no use."

How did I know all this? I hadn't known it before; not really, not the way I did then, with absolute certainty. But it was true. It is true. She didn't kill him and neither did I. She gave us those caring projects because she cared about us. She was trying to teach us something. It went wrong for us but it wasn't a bad idea. What was in me then, knowing all that and telling it to her, was more than just me. It was David too.

His was the impulse to heal, always. Make it better, care. David would not have let Mrs. Fulton go on suffering without trying to help. It was his way to reach out to hurt and try to ease it. And now it is mine too. This is what I have left. It is what he gave me.

I remembered suddenly what David had said about sex that day in class. 'His recipe' Helen had called it. Sex is in the joining, the mixing, the blending of two people. He'd known that from the very start, before Mrs. Fulton, before any of it. And it was me he shared himself with. Me. He picked me out of all the world to love and I loved him too. We had that. I've spent months regretting that we never had sex, that we spent so much time thinking about Maggie, taking care of her, that we didn't make enough time for each other. Not enough to have sex. But now I see that we were joined; sex or no sex, he is in me still.

We sat together for what seems a long time. For a while she cried and then I cried too. I haven't cried much in all this time and it hurt. When the tears began to fall, they burned my cheeks. I felt a terrible pressure inside my head, behind my eyes; it hurt. But slowly it eased, there was some relief. Mrs. Fulton came over to where I sat by the window and hugged me. No one has touched me much this past year, and I wasn't used to it. It made me cry harder at first.

"What's that?" she asked at last.

"What?" I didn't know what she was talking about.

"That," she said indicating the chain around my neck.

And I began to smile. Slowly I pulled it out and showed it to her. "This is Saint Jude. He's the saint of impossible causes."

I saw a slow, puzzled smile come into her eyes.

"David gave it to me at Christmas, last year."

"Impossible causes?" she asked.

"Yes."

"I suppose someone has to look after those," she said slowly.

"Yes. And he looks after me."

"Are you an impossible cause?" she asked gently.

"I don't know. I didn't used to be. At least David said I wasn't, but now, I don't know. I think I may be." So many words — perhaps crying had loosened them. I wanted to talk to her. I trusted her. So I said it. "I don't want to get better, Mrs. Fulton. I'm afraid to."

"You are? Why?"

Such a simple question and suddenly I knew the answer. "If I get better I'd be leaving him. Alone. Leaving David to die by himself." I began to cry again. She had her arm around me and tightened her hold.

"Well, I don't think you ever will get better, Olivia," she said after a while, "not all the way. I suppose Dr.

Hirsch would rather I not say that but it's what I think."

"You don't?" Her saying that made me feel much lighter.

"No. You'll never get over this. Not completely anyway. You couldn't. You'll never be the same, never be young again. You'll never be in love for the first time again. All of that is behind you now."

In the hall outside my room I heard the nurse's aide calling us out for dinner. I knew Mrs. Fulton would have to leave soon. She heard it too, but made no move. "I'm thinking of the tree outside my window, Liv. At school. Do you know which one I mean?" she asked.

I shook my head, but then I did know. "Yes. That old oak you always stare at."

"Yes. That's the one. It's what you remind me of."

"I do?"

"Olivia, can you see that tree? Right now, can you see it?"

"Yes." And I could.

"You know how old it is? How gnarled and twisted? Can you see it?" I nodded. "That tree has been hurt, Livvie. Branches have been blown off, limbs torn away. I don't know what all happened to it, but I can see it's been hurt. And yet somehow it's kept on growing. Perhaps life is a habit if nothing else. The hurt places still show. The scars are there and they will always be there. But it lives on. Scarred but still growing. That's what I see when I look at you."

And then it was time for her to leave.

I imagine I look the same as I did this morning. But I am not, Hirsch. Something is better. I too am a twisted oak, living on. And in me, warming my bones, is David. I am going to go on. With him and without him.

Both David and Mrs. Fulton taught me a lot about caring. About sex. About love. I taught myself about pain. It has to mean something, to be put to use, caring use. Otherwise it just kills you. And I don't want to die.